A SHOCKER ON SHOCK STREET

Goosebumps®

A SHOCKER ON SHOCK STREET

R.L. STINE

SCHOLASTIC INC.
New York Toronto London Auckland Sydney
Mexico City New Delhi Hong Kong Buenos Aires

12 11 10 9 8 7 6 5 4 3 2 1   3 4 5 6 7 8/0

Printed in the U.S.A.   40

First Scholastic printing, September 1995

"This is creepy, Erin." My friend Marty grabbed my sleeve.

"Let go!" I whispered. "You're hurting me!"

Marty didn't seem to hear. He stared straight ahead into the darkness, gripping my arm.

"Marty, please — " I whispered. I shook my arm free. I was scared, too. But I didn't want to admit it.

It was darker than the darkest night. I squinted hard, trying to see. And then a gray light glowed dimly in front of us.

Marty ducked low. Even in the foggy light, I could see the fear in his eyes.

He grabbed my arm again. His mouth dropped open. I could hear him breathing hard and fast.

Even though I was frightened, a smile crossed my face. I *liked* seeing Marty scared.

I really enjoyed it.

I know, I know. That's terrible. I admit it. Erin

Wright is a bad person. What kind of a friend am I?

But Marty always brags that he is braver than me. And he is usually right. He usually *is* the brave one, and I'm the wimp.

But not today.

That's why seeing Marty gasp in fright and grab my arm made me smile.

The gray light ahead of us slowly grew brighter. I heard crunching sounds on both sides of us. Close behind me, someone coughed. But Marty and I didn't turn around. We kept our eyes straight ahead.

Waiting. Watching. . . .

As I squinted into the gray light, a fence came into view. A long wooden fence, its paint faded and peeling. A hand-lettered sign appeared on the fence: DANGER. KEEP OUT. THIS MEANS YOU.

Marty and I both gasped when we heard the scraping sounds. Soft at first. Then louder. Like giant claws scraping against the other side of the fence.

I tried to swallow, but my mouth suddenly felt dry. I had the urge to run. Just turn and run as fast as I could.

But I couldn't leave Marty there all alone. And besides, if I ran away now, he would never let me forget it. He'd tease me about it forever.

2

So I stayed beside him, listening as the scraping, clawing sounds turned into banging. Loud crashes.

Was someone trying to break through the fence?

We moved quickly along the fence. Faster, faster — until the tall, peeling fence pickets became a gray blur.

But the sound followed us. Heavy footsteps on the other side of the fence.

We stared straight ahead. We were on an empty street. A familiar street.

Yes, we had been here before.

The pavement was puddled with rainwater. The puddles glowed in the pale light from the streetlamps.

I took a deep breath. Marty gripped my arm harder. Our mouths gaped open.

To our horror, the fence began to shake. The whole street shook. The rain puddles splashed against the curb.

The footsteps thundered closer.

"Marty — !" I gasped in a choked whisper.

Before I could say another word, the fence crumbled to the ground, and the monster came bursting out.

It had a head like a wolf — snapping jaws of gleaming white teeth — and a body like a giant crab. It swung four huge claws in front of it, clicking them at us as its snout pulled open in a throaty growl.

"NOOOOOOO!" Marty and I both let out howls of terror.

We jumped to our feet.

But there was nowhere to run.

2

We stood and stared as the wolf-crab crawled toward us.

"Please sit down, kids," a voice called out behind us. "I can't see the screen."

"Ssshhhh!" someone else whispered.

Marty and I glanced at each other. I guess we both felt like jerks. I know I did. We dropped back into our seats.

And watched the wolf-crab scamper across the street, chasing after a little boy on a tricycle.

"What's your problem, Erin?" Marty whispered, shaking his head. "It's only a movie. Why did you scream like that?"

"You screamed too!" I replied sharply.

"I only screamed because you screamed!" he insisted.

"Sssshhh!" someone pleaded. I sank low in the seat. I heard crunching sounds all around me. People eating popcorn. Someone behind me coughed.

On the screen, the wolf-crab reached out his big, red claws and grabbed the kid on the trike. *SNAP. SNAP.* Good-bye, kid.

Some people in the theater laughed. It *was* pretty funny.

That's the great thing about the *Shocker on Shock Street* movies. They make you scream and laugh at the same time.

Marty and I sat back and enjoyed the rest of the movie. We love scary movies, but the *Shock Street* films are our favorites.

In the end, the police caught the wolf-crab. They boiled him in a big pot of water. Then they served steamed crab to the whole town. Everyone sat around dipping him in butter sauce. They all said he was delicious.

It was the perfect ending. Marty and I clapped and cheered. Marty put two fingers in his mouth and whistled through his teeth the way he always does.

We had just seen *Shocker on Shock Street VI,* and it was definitely the best one of the series.

The theater lights came on. We turned up the aisle and started to make our way through the crowd.

"Great special effects," a man told his friend.

"Special effects?" the friend replied. "I thought it was all real!"

They both laughed.

Marty bumped me hard from behind. He thinks

it's funny to try and knock me over. "Pretty good movie," he said.

I turned back to him. "Huh? *Pretty* good?"

"Well, it wasn't scary enough," he replied. "Actually, it was kind of babyish. *Shocker V* was a lot scarier."

I rolled my eyes. "Marty, you screamed your head off — remember? You jumped out of your seat. You grabbed my arm and — "

"I only did that because I saw how scared you were," he said, grinning. What a liar! Why can't he ever admit it when he's scared?

He stuck his sneaker out and tried to trip me.

I dodged to the left, stumbled — and bumped hard into a young woman.

"Hey — look out!" she cried. "You twins should be more careful."

"We're not twins!" Marty and I cried in unison.

We're not even brother and sister. We're not related in any way. But people always think that Marty and I are twins.

I guess we do look a lot alike. We're both twelve years old. And we're both pretty short and kind of chubby. We both have round faces, short black hair, and blue eyes. And we both have little noses that sort of turn up.

But we're not twins! We're only friends.

I apologized to the woman. When I turned back to Marty, he stuck out his shoe and tried to trip me again.

7

I stumbled, but quickly caught my balance. Then I stuck out my shoe — and tripped him.

We kept tripping each other through the long lobby. People were staring at us, but we didn't care. We were laughing too hard.

"Do you know the coolest thing about this movie?" I asked.

"No. What?"

"That we're the first kids in the world to see it!" I exclaimed.

"Yeah!" Marty and I slapped each other a high five.

We had just seen *Shocker on Shock Street VI* at a special sneak preview. My dad works with a lot of movie people, and he got us tickets for it. The others in the theater were all adults. Marty and I were the only kids.

"Know what else was really cool?" I asked. "The monsters. All of them. They looked so incredibly real. It didn't look like special effects at all."

Marty frowned. "Well, I thought the Electric Eel Woman was pretty phony-looking. She didn't look like an eel — she looked like a big worm!"

I laughed. "Then why did you jump out of your seat when she shot a bolt of electricity and fried that gang of teenagers?"

"I didn't jump," Marty insisted. "*You* did!"

"Did not! You jumped because it looked so real," I insisted. "And I heard you choke when the Toxic Creep leaped out of the nuclear waste pit."

"I choked on a Milk Dud, that's all."

"You were scared, Marty, because it was so real."

"Hey — what if they *are* real?!" Marty exclaimed. "What if it isn't special effects? What if they're all *real monsters*?"

"Don't be dumb," I said.

We turned the corner into another hall.

The wolf-crab stood waiting for me there.

I didn't even have time to scream.

He opened his toothy jaws in a long wolf howl — and wrapped two giant red claws around my waist.

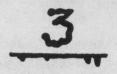

I opened my mouth to scream, but only a squeak came out.

I heard people laughing.

The big claws slid off my waist. Plastic claws.

I saw two dark eyes staring out at me from behind the wolf mask. I should have known that it was a man in a costume. But I didn't expect him to be standing there.

I was surprised, that's all.

I blinked at a white flash of light. A man had just taken a picture of the creature. I saw a big red and yellow sign against the wall: SEE THE MOVIE — THEN PLAY THE GAME ON CD-ROM.

"Sorry if I scared you," the man inside the wolf-crab costume said softly.

"She scares easily!" Marty declared.

I gave Marty a hard shove, and we hurried away. I turned back to see the creature waving a claw at me. "We've got to go upstairs and see my dad," I told Marty.

"Tell me something I *don't* know."

He thinks he's so funny.

Dad's office is upstairs from the theater, on the twenty-ninth floor. We jogged to the elevators at the end of the hall and took one up.

Dad has a really cool job. He builds theme parks. And he designs all kinds of rides.

Dad was one of the designers of Prehistoric Park. That's the big theme park where you go back to prehistoric times. It has all kinds of neat rides and shows — and dozens of huge dinosaur robots wandering around.

And Dad worked on the Fantasy Films Studio Tour. Everyone who comes to Hollywood goes on that tour.

Dad's idea was the part where you walk through a huge movie screen and find yourself in a world of movie characters. You can star in any kind of movie you want to be in!

I know it sounds as if I'm bragging, but Dad is really smart, and he's an engineering genius! I think he is the world expert on robots. He can build robots that will do anything! And he uses them in all his parks and studio tours.

Marty and I stepped off the elevator on the twenty-ninth floor. We waved to the woman at the front desk. Then we hurried to Dad's office at the end of the hall.

It looks more like a playroom than an office. It's a big room. Huge, really. Filled with toys, and stuffed cartoon characters, movie posters, and models of monsters.

Marty and I love to roam around the office, staring at all the neat stuff. On the walls, Dad has great posters from a dozen different movies. On a long table, he has a model of The Tumbler, the upside-down roller coaster he designed. The model has little cars that really screech around the tracks.

And he has a lot of cool stuff from *Shock Street* — like one of the original furry paws that Wolf Girl wore in *Nightmare on Shock Street*. He keeps it in a glass case on the windowsill.

He has models of tramcars and little trains and planes and rockets. Even a big, silver plastic blimp. It's radio-controlled, and he can make it float round and around his office.

What a great place! I always think of Dad's office as the happiest place in the world.

But today, as Marty and I stepped inside, Dad didn't look too happy. He hunched over his desk with the telephone to his ear. His head was lowered, his eyes down. He kept a hand pressed against his forehead as he mumbled into the phone.

Dad and I don't look at all alike. I'm short and dark. He's tall and thin. And he has blond hair, although there's not much left of it. He's pretty bald.

He has the kind of skin that turns red easily.

His cheeks get real pink when he talks. And he wears big, round glasses with dark frames that hide his brown eyes.

Marty and I stopped at the doorway. I don't think Dad saw us. He stared down at the desk. He had his tie pulled down and his shirt collar open.

He muttered for a short while longer. Marty and I crept into the office.

Finally, Dad set down the phone. He raised his eyes and saw us. "Oh, hi, you two," he said softly. His cheeks turned bright pink.

"Dad — what's wrong?" I asked.

He sighed. Then he pulled off his glasses and pinched the bridge of his nose. "I have very bad news, Erin. Very bad news."

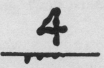

4

"Dad — what is it? *What?*" I cried.

Then I saw the grin slowly spread across his face. I knew I'd been tricked again.

"Gotcha!" he declared. His brown eyes flashed gleefully. His cheeks were bright pink. "Gotcha again. You fall for that gag every time."

"Dad — !" I let out an angry cry. Then I rushed up to the desk, wrapped my hands around his neck, and pretended to strangle him.

We both collapsed against each other, laughing. Marty still stood in the doorway, shaking his head. "Mr. Wright, that is so lame," he muttered.

Dad struggled to slip his glasses back on. "I'm sorry. You kids are just too easy to fool. I couldn't resist." He smiled at me. "Actually, I've got *good* news."

"Good news? Is this another joke?" I demanded suspiciously.

He shook his head. He picked up something

from his desk. "Check this out, guys. Do you know what this is?" He held it in his palm.

Marty and I came closer to examine it. It was a little, white plastic vehicle with four wheels. "Some kind of train car?" I guessed.

"It's a tramcar," Dad explained. "See? People sit on long benches inside it. Here. It's motor-driven." He pointed to the front of the model to show where the engine went. "But, do you know *where* this tramcar will be used?"

"Dad, we give up. Just *tell* us," I insisted impatiently. "Stop keeping us in suspense."

"Okay, okay." His cheeks reddened. His smile grew wider. "This is a model of the tram that will be used at the Shocker Studio Tour."

My mouth dropped open. "Do you mean the tour is finally going to open?" I knew that Dad had been working on it for years.

Dad nodded. "Yes. We're finally about to open it to the public. But before we do, I want you two to test it out."

"Huh? You *mean* it?" I shrieked. I was so excited, I felt as if I'd burst out of my skin!

I turned to Marty. He was leaping up and down, shooting both fists into the air. "Yes! Yes! Yes!"

"I built this whole tour," Dad said, "and I want you two to be the first kids in the world to go on it. I want to know your opinion. What you like and what you don't like."

"Yes! Yes! Yes!" Marty kept leaping into the air. I thought I might have to tie a rope around his waist and hold onto it to keep him from floating away!

"Dad — the *Shock Street* movies are the *best!*" I cried. "This is awesome!" And then I added, "Is the tour very scary?"

Dad rested a hand on my shoulder. "I hope so," he replied. "I tried to make it as scary and real as I could. You get on the tram and you ride through the whole movie studio. You get to meet all of the characters from the horror movies. And then the tram takes you on a slow ride down Shock Street."

"The *real* Shock Street?" Marty cried. "Do you mean it? You get to ride down the real street where they make the movies?"

Dad nodded. "Yes. The real Shock Street."

"Yes! Yes! Yes!" Marty started pumping his fists in the air again, shouting like a maniac.

"Awesome!" I cried. "Totally awesome!" I was as excited as Marty.

Suddenly Marty stopped leaping. His expression turned serious. "Maybe Erin shouldn't go," he told my dad. "She gets too scared."

"Huh?" I cried.

"She was so scared during the movie sneak preview, I had to hold her hand," Marty told Dad.

What a liar!

"Give me a break!" I cried angrily. "If anyone was a scaredy-cat wimp, it was you, Marty!"

Dad raised both hands to signal *halt*. "Calm down, guys," he said softly. "No arguing. You have to keep together. You know, you two will be the *only* ones on the tour tomorrow. The only ones."

"Yes!" Marty cheered happily. "Yes! Yes!"

"Wow! That's great!" I cried. "It's totally great. It's going to be the *best*!" Then I had an idea. "Can Mom come too? I bet she would really enjoy it."

"Excuse me?" Dad squinted at me through his glasses. His whole face turned bright red. "What did you say?"

"I asked if Mom could come too," I repeated.

Dad kept staring at me for a long time, studying me. "Are you feeling okay, Erin?" he asked finally.

"Yes. Fine," I replied meekly.

I suddenly felt very confused and upset. What had I done wrong?

Was something wrong with Mom?

Why was Dad staring at me like that?

5

Dad came around the desk and put an arm around my shoulder. "I think you and Marty will have a better time if you go by yourselves," he said softly. "Don't you agree?"

I nodded. "Yeah. I guess."

I still wondered why he was staring at me so suspiciously. But I decided not to ask him. I didn't want him to get angry or something and change his mind about us going on the tour.

"Do you mean you're not coming with us?" Marty asked Dad. "We're really going by ourselves?"

"I want you to go by yourselves," Dad replied. "I think that will make it more exciting for you."

Marty grinned at me. "I hope it's really scary!" he declared.

"Don't worry," Dad replied. A strange smile spread over his face. "You won't be disappointed."

The next afternoon, a gray haze hung in the air as Dad drove Marty and me to Shocker Studios.

I sat up front with Dad, peering out the car window at the smog. "It's so gloomy out," I murmured.

"Perfect for a horror movie tour," Marty chimed in from the backseat. He was so excited, he could barely sit still. He kept bouncing his legs up and down and tapping his hands on the leather seat.

I had never seen Marty so crazed. If he didn't have his seat belt to hold him down, he'd probably bounce right out of the car!

The car climbed up the Hollywood hills. The narrow road curved past redwood houses and tree-filled yards cut into the sides of the hills.

As we climbed, the sky turned even darker. We're driving up into a cloud of fog, I thought. Far in the distance, I could see the HOLLY-WOOD sign, stretching in the haze across a dark peak.

"Hope it doesn't rain," I muttered, watching the fog roll over the sign.

Dad chuckled. "You know it *never* rains in Los Angeles!"

"Which monsters are we going to see?" Marty asked, bouncing in the backseat. "Is Shockro on the tour? Do we really get to walk on Shock Street?"

Dad squinted hard through his glasses, turning the wheel as the road curved and twisted. "I'm not telling," he replied. "I don't want to spoil it for you. I want it all to be a surprise."

"I just wanted to know so I could warn Erin," Marty said. "I don't want her to get too scared. She might faint or something." He laughed.

I let out an angry growl. Then I turned around and tried to punch him. But I couldn't reach.

Marty leaned forward and messed up my hair with both hands. "Get off me!" I screamed. "I'm warning you — !"

"Take it easy, guys," Dad said softly. "We're here."

I turned and stared out the windshield. The road had flattened out. Up ahead, an enormous sign proclaimed SHOCKER STUDIOS in scary, blood-red letters.

We drove slowly up to the huge iron gates in the front. The gates were closed. A guard in a small black booth sat reading a newspaper. I glimpsed gold script letters above the gate. They spelled out one word: BEWARE.

Dad pulled right up to the gate, and the guard peered up. He gave Dad a big smile. Then he pressed a button, and the gates slowly swung open. Dad drove the car into the tall white parking garage beside the studio. He parked in the first space next to the entrance. The garage seemed to stretch on forever. But I could see only three or four other cars inside.

"When we open next week, this garage will be jammed!" Dad said. "There will be thousands of people here. I hope."

"And today, we're the only ones!" Marty cried excitedly, jumping out of the car.

"We're so lucky!" I agreed.

A few minutes later, we were standing on the platform outside the main building, facing a wide street, waiting for the tram to take us on the tour. The street led to dozens of white studio buildings, spread out all the way down the hill.

Dad pointed to two enormous buildings as big as airplane hangars. "Those are the soundstages," he explained. "They film a lot of movie scenes inside those buildings."

"Does the tour go inside them?" Marty demanded. "Where is Shock Street? Where are the monsters? Are they making a movie now? Can we watch them making it?"

"Whoa!" Dad cried. He placed his hands on Marty's shoulders as if to keep him from flying off the ground. I had never seen Marty so totally wired! "Take it easy, fella," Dad warned. "You'll blow a fuse! You won't survive the tour!"

I shook my head. "Maybe we should put him on a leash," I told Dad.

"Arf, arf!" Marty barked. Then he snapped his teeth at me, trying to bite me.

I shivered. The fog rolled in from the hills. The air felt damp and cold. The sky darkened.

Two men in business suits came zooming along the street in a golf cart. They were both talking at once. One of them waved to Dad.

"Can we ride in one of those carts?" Marty asked. "Can Erin and I each have our own cart?"

"No way," Dad told him. "You have to take the automated tram. And remember — stay in the tramcar. No matter what."

"You mean we can't walk on Shock Street?" Marty whined.

Dad shook his head. "Not allowed. You have to stay on the tram."

He turned to me. "I'll be waiting for you here on the platform when you get back. I want a full report. I want to know what you like and what you don't like. And don't worry if things don't work exactly right. There are still a few bugs to work out."

"Hey — here comes the tram!" Marty cried, hopping up and down and pointing.

The tram came rolling silently around the corner. I counted six tramcars in all. They were shaped like roller-coaster cars, open on top — only much longer and wider. The cars were black. A grinning white skull was painted on the front of the first car.

A young, red-haired woman wearing a black uniform was seated on the first bench in the front car. She waved to us as the tram rolled up to the platform. She was the only passenger.

She hopped out as the tram stopped. "Hi, I'm Linda. I'm your tour guide." She smiled at my dad. Her red hair fluttered in the wind.

"Hello, Linda," Dad said, smiling back at her. He gently shoved Marty and me forward. "Here are your first two victims."

Linda laughed and asked us our names. We told her.

"Can we ride in front?" Marty asked eagerly.

"Yes, of course," Linda replied. "You can sit anywhere you want. This whole ride is just for you."

"All right!" Marty cried. He slapped me a high five.

Dad laughed. "I think Marty is ready to begin," he told Linda.

Linda pushed her red hair out of her face. "You can start right away, guys. But first, there's something I have to do."

She leaned over the tramcar and tugged out a black canvas bag. "This will only take a second, guys." She pulled a red plastic gun from the bag. "This is a Shocker Stun Ray Blaster."

She gripped the plastic pistol tightly. It looked like something in a *Star Trek* movie. Her smile faded. Her green eyes narrowed. "Be careful with these blasters, guys. They can freeze a monster in its tracks from twenty feet."

She handed the blaster to me. Then she reached into her bag to get one for Marty. "Don't fire them unless you have to." She swallowed hard and bit her lower lip. "I sure hope you don't have to."

I laughed. "You're kidding — right? These are just toys — right?"

She didn't answer. She pulled another blaster from her bag and started to bring it to Marty.

But she stumbled over a cord on the platform. "Ohh!" She let out a startled cry as the blaster went off in her hand.

A loud buzz. A bright ray of yellow light.

And Linda stood frozen on the platform.

6

"Linda! Linda!" I screamed.

Marty's mouth dropped open. He let out a choked gurgle.

I turned to Dad. To my surprise, he was laughing.

"Dad — she's — she's frozen!" I cried. But when I turned back to Linda, she had a big smile on her face, too.

It took us both a while, but we soon realized the whole thing was a joke.

"That's the first shock on the *Shocker* tour," Linda announced, lowering the red blaster. She put a hand on Marty's shoulder. "I think I really shocked *you*, Marty!"

"No way!" Marty insisted. "I knew it was a joke. I just played along."

"Come on, Marty!" I cried, rolling my eyes. "You nearly dropped your teeth!"

"Erin, I *wasn't* scared," Marty insisted sharply. "Really. I just went along with the joke. Do you really think I'd fall for a dumb plastic blaster gun?"

Marty is such a jerk. Why can't he ever admit it when he's scared?

"Climb in, you two," Dad urged. "Let's get this show on the road."

Marty and I climbed into the front seat of the tram. I looked for a seat belt or a safety bar, but there wasn't one. "Are you coming with us?" I asked Linda.

She shook her head. "No. You're on your own. The tram moves automatically." She handed Marty his Stun Blaster. "Hope you don't need it."

"Yeah. Sure," Marty muttered, rolling his eyes. "This gun is so babyish."

"Remember — I'll meet you back here at the end of the ride," Dad said. He waved. "Enjoy it. I want a full report."

"Don't get out of the tram," Linda reminded us. "Keep your head and arms inside. And don't stand up while the tram is moving."

She stepped on a blue button on the platform. The tram started up with a jolt. Marty and I were thrown back against the seat. Then the tram rolled smoothly forward.

"First stop is The Haunted House of Horror!" Linda called after us. "Good luck!"

I turned back to see her waving to us, her long red hair fluttering in the wind. A strong breeze blew against us as the tram made its way down the hill. The sky was nearly as dark as night. Some of the white studio buildings were hidden by the fog.

"Stupid gun," Marty muttered, rolling it around in his hands. "Why do we need this plastic gun? I hope the whole tour isn't this babyish."

"I hope you don't complain all afternoon," I told him, frowning. "Do you realize how awesome this is? We're going to see all the great creatures from the *Shocker* movies."

"Think we'll see Shockro?" he asked. Shockro is his favorite. I guess because he's so totally gross.

"Probably," I replied, my eyes on the low buildings we were passing. They all stood dark and empty.

"I want to see Wolf Boy and Wolf Girl," Marty said, counting the monsters off on his fingers. "And . . . the Piranha People, and Captain Sick, The Great Gopher Mutant, and — "

"Wow! Look!" I cried, pounding his shoulder and pointing.

As the tram turned a sharp corner, The Haunted House of Horror loomed darkly in front of us. The roof and its tall stone turrets were hidden by the fog. The rest of the mansion stood gray against the dusky sky.

The tram took us nearer. Tall weeds choked the front lawn. The weeds bent and swayed in the wind. The gray shingles on the house were chipped and peeling. Pale green light, dim, eerie light, floated out from the tall window in front.

As we rode closer, I could see a rusty iron porch swing — swinging by itself! — on a broken, rotting porch.

"Cool!" I exclaimed.

"It looks a lot smaller than in the movie," Marty grumbled.

"It's exactly the same house!" I cried.

"Then why does it look so much smaller?" he demanded.

What a complainer.

I turned away from him and studied The Haunted House. An iron fence surrounded the place. As we moved around to the side, the rusty gate swung open, squeaking and creaking.

"Look!" I pointed to the dark windows on the second floor. The shutters all flew open at once, then banged shut again.

Lights came on in the windows. Through the window shades, I could see the silhouettes of skeletons hanging, swinging slowly back and forth.

"That's kind of cool," Marty said. "But not too scary." He raised his plastic gun and pretended to shoot at the skeletons.

We circled The Haunted House of Horror once. We could hear screams of terror from inside. The shutters banged again and again. The porch swing continued to creak back and forth, back and forth, as if taken by a ghost.

"Are we going inside or not?" Marty demanded impatiently.

"Sit back and stop complaining," I said sharply. "The ride just started. Don't spoil it for me, okay?"

He stuck his tongue out at me. But he settled back against the seat. We heard a long howl, and then a shrill scream of horror.

The tram made its way silently to the back of the house. A gate swung open and we rolled through it. We moved quickly through the overgrown, weed-choked backyard.

The tram picked up speed. We bounced over the lawn. Up to the back door. A wooden sign above the door read: ABANDON ALL HOPE.

We're going to crash right into the door! I thought. I ducked and raised my hands to shield myself.

But the door creaked open, and we burst inside.

The tram slowed. I lowered my hands and sat up. We were in a dark, dust-covered kitchen. An invisible ghost cackled, an evil laugh. Battered pots and pans covered the wall. As we passed, they clattered to the floor.

The oven door opened and closed by itself. The teapot on the stove started to whistle. Dishes on the shelves rattled. The cackling grew louder.

"This is pretty creepy," I whispered.

"Ooh. Thrills and chills!" Marty replied sarcastically. He crossed his arms in front of him. "Bor-ring!"

"Marty — give me a break." I shoved him away. "You can be a bad sport if you want. But don't ruin it for me."

That seemed to get to him. He muttered, "Sorry," and scooted back next to me.

The tram moved out of the dark kitchen, into an even darker hallway. Paintings of goblins and ugly creatures hung on the hallway walls.

As we approached a closet door, it sprang open — and a shrieking skeleton popped out in front of us, its jaws open, its arms jutting out to grab us.

I screamed. Marty laughed.

The skeleton snapped back into the closet. The tram turned a corner. I saw flickering light up ahead.

We rode into a large, round room. "It's the living room," I whispered to Marty. I raised my eyes to the flickering light and saw a chandelier above our heads, with a dozen burning candles.

The tram stopped beneath it. The chandelier began to shake. Then, with a hiss, the candles all flickered out at once.

The room plunged into darkness.

Then a deep laugh echoed all around us.

I gasped.

"Welcome to my humble home!" a deep voice suddenly boomed.

"Who is that?" I whispered to Marty. "Where is it coming from?"

No reply.

"Hey — Marty?"

I turned to him. "Marty — ?"

He was gone.

7

"Marty?"

My breath caught in my throat. I froze, staring into the darkness.

Where did he go? I asked myself. He knows we aren't supposed to leave the tramcar. Did he climb out?

No.

If he had, I would have heard him.

"Marty?"

Someone grabbed my arm.

I heard a soft laugh. Marty's laugh.

"Hey — where are you? I can't see you!" I cried.

"I can't see you, either," he replied. "But I didn't move. I'm still sitting right next to you."

"Huh?" I reached out and felt the sleeve of his shirt.

"This is cool!" Marty declared. "I'm waving my arms, but I can't see a thing. You really can't see me?"

"No," I replied. "I thought — "

"It's some kind of trick with the lights," he said. "Black light or something. Some kind of neat movie special effect."

"Well, it creeped me out," I confessed. "I really thought you disappeared."

"Sucker," he sneered.

And then we both jumped.

A fire suddenly blazed in the big brick fireplace. Bright orange light filled the room. A big black armchair spun around to reveal a grinning skeleton.

The skeleton raised its bony yellowed head. The jaws moved. *"I hope you like my house,"* its voice boomed. *"Because you will never leave!"*

It tossed back its head and let out an evil cackle.

The tram jolted to a start. We rumbled out of the living room. Into a long, dark hallway. The skeleton's laugh followed us into the hall.

I fell back against the seat as we picked up speed.

We whirred around a corner. Down another long hall, so dark I couldn't see the walls.

Faster. Faster.

We whipped around another corner. Made another sharp turn.

We were climbing now. And then we took a sharp dip that made both of us throw up our hands and scream.

Around another sharp turn. Up, up, up. And then we came crashing down.

A wild roller-coaster ride in total darkness.

It was awesome. Even better because we didn't expect it. Marty and I screamed our heads off. We bumped hard against each other as the tram whirled around in the black halls of The Haunted House of Horror. Up, up, again — then we tilted sharply down.

I hung on to the front of the car for dear life. I gripped it so hard, both hands ached. There was no seat belt, no safety bar.

What if we tumbled out? I wondered.

The car tilted sharply sideways, as if reading my frightened thoughts. I let out a shriek and lost my grip. I slid against the side of the car. Marty fell on top of me.

I frantically reached out for something to hold on to.

The car tilted back rightside up. I took a deep breath, slid back into place on the long seat.

"Whoa! That was *excellent!*" Marty cried, laughing. "Excellent!"

Gripping the front of the car, I took another deep breath and held it. I was trying to slow my racing heart.

A door swung open in front of us, and we burst through it.

The car bounced hard. I saw trees. The gray-fogged sky.

We were back outside. Racing through the backyard. Both of us were tossed from side to side as we roared over the weeds, zigzagging through the dark trees.

"Whoa! Stop!" I choked out. I couldn't catch my breath. The wind blew hard against my face. The tram clattered and squealed as we bumped over the rough ground.

We were out of control. Something had definitely gone wrong with the tram.

Bouncing hard on the plastic seat, holding on tightly, I searched for someone who could help us.

No one in sight.

We bumped onto the road. The tram started to slow. I turned to Marty. His hair was blown over his face. His mouth hung open. His eyes rolled around in his head. He was totally dazed.

The tram slowed, slowed, slowed, until we were creeping smoothly along.

"That was *great!*" Marty declared. He smoothed back his hair with both hands and grinned at me. I knew he had been scared, too. But he was pretending that he enjoyed the crazy, wild ride.

"Yeah. Great." I tried to pretend, too. But my voice came out weak and shaky.

"I'm going to tell your dad that the roller-coaster ride through the halls was the *best!*" Marty declared.

"It was kind of fun," I agreed. "And kind of scary."

Marty turned away from me. "Hey. Where are we?"

The tram had come to a stop. I pulled myself up and peered around. We had parked between two rows of tall evergreen bushes. The bushes were slender, shaped like spears reaching up to the sky.

Above us, the afternoon sun was trying to break through the fog. Rays of pale light beamed down from the gray sky. The tall, thin shadows of the bushes fell over our tramcar.

Marty stood up and turned to the back of the tram. "There's nothing around here," he said. "We're in the middle of nowhere. Why did we stop?"

"Do you think — ?" I started. But I stopped talking when I saw the bush move.

It wiggled. Then the bush next to it wiggled, too.

"Marty — " I whispered, tugging his sleeve. I saw two glowing red circles behind the bush. Two glowing red *eyes*!

"Marty — there's someone there."

Another pair of eyes. And then another pair of eyes. Staring out at us from behind the evergreen bushes.

And then two dark claws.

And then rustling sounds. The bush tilted as a dark figure leaped out. Followed by another.

Snarling, growling.

I gasped. Too late to run.

We were surrounded by the ugly creatures. Snuffling, wheezing creatures, who staggered out from the bushes. Reaching out, reaching out for us, they began to climb into the tram.

Marty and I jumped to our feet.

"Ohhhhhh." I heard Marty let out a frightened moan.

I started to back away. I thought maybe I could scramble out the other side of the car.

But the snarling, growling monsters came at us from both sides.

"L-leave us alone!" I stammered.

A monster covered in tangled brown fur opened his jaws to reveal long, jagged rows of yellow teeth. His hot breath exploded in my face. He stepped closer. Then he swiped at me with a fat paw and uttered a menacing roar. "Would you like an autograph?" he growled.

I gaped at him, my mouth hanging down to my knees. "Huh?"

"Autographed photo?" he asked. He raised his furry paw again. He held a black-and-white snapshot in it.

"Hey — you're Ape Face!" Marty cried, pointing.

The hairy creature nodded his head. He raised the photo to Marty. "Want a photo? This is the autographing part of the tour."

"Yeah! Okay," Marty replied.

The big ape pulled a marker from behind his ear and bent to sign the photo for Marty.

Now that my heartbeat was returning to normal, I began to recognize some of the other creatures. The guy covered in purple slime was The Toxic Wild Man. And I recognized Sweet Sue, the walking-talking baby doll with real hair you can brush. Sweet Sue was really a mutant murderer from Mars.

The frog-faced guy covered from head to toe with purple and brown warts was The Fabulous Frog, also known as The Toadinator. He starred in *Pond Scum* and *Pond Scum II*, two of the scariest movies ever made.

"Frog — can I have your autograph?" I asked.

"Grrrbbit. Grrbit." He croaked and slipped a pen into his wart-covered hand. I leaned forward eagerly and watched him sign his photo. It was hard for him to write. The pen kept slipping in his slimy frog hands.

Marty and I collected a bunch of autographs. Then the creatures went snarling and wheezing back into the bushes.

When they were gone, we both burst out laughing. "That was so dumb!" I cried. "When I saw them creeping out from behind the bushes, I thought I'd have a cow!" I glanced down at the photos. "But it's kind of cool to get their autographs."

Marty made a disgusted face. "It's just a bunch of actors in costumes," he sneered. "It's for babies."

"But — but — they looked so real," I stammered. "It didn't look as if they were wearing costumes — did it? I mean, The Toadinator's hands were really slimy. And Ape Face's fur was so real. The masks were awesome. I couldn't tell they were masks."

I brushed the hair out of my eyes. "How do they get into those costumes? I didn't see any buttons or zippers, or anything!"

"That's because they're movie costumes," Marty explained. "They're better than regular costumes."

Mr. Know-It-All.

The tram started to back out. I settled down into the seat. I watched the two rows of evergreen bushes fade into the distance.

Down the long, sloping hill, I could see the white studio buildings. I wondered if they were making a movie on one of the soundstages. I wondered if the tram would take us to watch them shoot.

I could see two golf carts moving along the road.

40

They were carrying people down to the sound-stage buildings.

The sun still struggled to shine through the fog. The tram bounced over the grass, up the hill.

"Whoa!" I cried out as we turned sharply and headed back toward the trees.

"Please remain in the car at all times." A woman's voice burst from a speaker in the tram car. "Your next stop will be The Cave of The Living Creeps."

"The Cave of The Living Creeps? Wow! That sounds scary!" Marty exclaimed.

"Sure does!" I agreed.

We had no idea just how scary it would turn out to be.

9

The tram zigzagged its way through the trees. Their shadows rolled over us like dark ghosts.

We moved so silently. I tried to imagine what the ride would be like if the tram was packed with excited kids and adults. I decided it would be a lot less scary with a crowd.

But I wasn't complaining. Marty and I were really lucky to be the first kids ever to try out this ride.

"Wow!" Marty grabbed my arm as The Cave of The Living Creeps loomed in front of us. The mouth of the cave was a huge dark hole, cut into the side of the hill. I could see pale, silvery light flickering past the entrance.

The tram slowed down as we approached the dark opening. A sign above the entrance had one word carved roughly into it: FAREWELL.

The tramcar lurched forward. "Hey — !" I cried out and ducked my head. What a tight squeeze!

Into the dim, flickering light.

The air instantly grew colder. And damp. A sour, earthy smell rose to my nostrils, making me gasp.

"Bats!" Marty whispered. "What do you think, Erin? Think there are bats in here?" He leaned close and let out an evil laugh in my ear.

Marty *knows* that I hate bats!

I know, I know. Bats aren't really evil creatures. And they aren't dangerous. Bats eat mosquitoes and other insects. And they don't attack people or get tangled in your hair or try to suck your blood. That's only in movies.

I know all that. But I don't care.

Bats are ugly and creepy and disgusting. And I hate them.

One day, I told Marty how much I hate bats. And so he's been teasing me about them ever since.

The tram moved deeper into the cave. The air grew colder. The sour aroma nearly choked me.

"Look — over there!" Marty screamed. "A vampire bat!"

"Huh? Where?" I couldn't help myself. I cried out in alarm.

Of course it was one of Marty's dumb jokes. He laughed like a maniac.

I growled at him and punched him hard on the shoulder. "You're not funny. You're just dumb."

That made him giggle even harder. "I'll bet

43

there *are* bats in this cave," he insisted. "You can't go into a deep, dark cave like this one without seeing bats."

I turned away from his grinning face and listened hard. I was listening for fluttering bat wings. I didn't hear any.

The cave narrowed. The walls seemed to close in on us. The side of the car scraped against the dirt wall. I could feel that we were heading down.

In the dim, silvery light, I saw a long row of pointy icicle-type things hanging down from the cave ceiling. I know they have a name, but I can never remember which one it is — stalagmites or stalactites.

I ducked my head again as the tram shot under them. Up close, they looked like pointed elephant tusks.

"We're getting closer to the bats!" Marty teased.

I ignored him. I kept my eyes straight ahead. The cave grew wide again. Dark shadows shifted and danced over the walls as we rolled past.

"Ohhh." I uttered a groan as I felt something cold and slimy drop onto the back of my neck.

I jerked away and turned sharply to Marty. "Cut it out!" I snapped. "Get your cold hands off me!"

"Who — me?"

He wasn't touching me. Both of his hands gripped the front of the car.

Then *what* was on the back of my neck? So cold and wet. Icy wet. I shuddered. My whole body shook.

"M-Marty!" I stammered. "H-help!"

Marty stared at me, confused. "Erin — what's your problem?"

"The back of my neck — " I choked out.

I could feel the cold, wet thing start to move. I decided not to wait for Marty to help me.

I reached back and pulled it off. It felt sticky and cold between my fingers. It slithered and wriggled, and I dropped it on the seat.

A worm!

A huge, long white worm. So cold, so wet and cold.

"Weird!" Marty exclaimed. He leaned close to examine it. "I've never seen a worm that big! And it's white."

"It — it dropped from the ceiling," I said, watching it wiggle next to me. "It's ice-cold."

"Huh? Let me touch it," Marty said. He raised his hand and slowly lowered his pointer finger to the worm.

His finger poked the worm in its middle.

And then Marty opened his mouth in a scream of horror that echoed through the cave.

10

"What is it? Marty — what's *wrong*?" I shrieked.

"I — I — I — " He couldn't speak. He could only utter, "I — I — I — !" His eyes bulged. His tongue flopped out.

He reached up and pulled a white worm off the top of his head. "I — I — I got one too!"

"Yuck!" I cried. His worm was nearly as long as a shoelace!

We both tossed our worms out of the tram.

But then I felt a soft, damp *plop* on my shoulder. And then a cold *plop* on top of my head. Another on my forehead, like a cold slap.

"Ohhh — help!" I moaned. I started thrashing my arms, grabbing at the worms, struggling to pull them off me.

"Marty — please!" I turned to him for help.

But he was battling them, too. Twisting and ducking. Trying to dodge, as more and more white worms fell from the ceiling.

I saw one fall on his shoulder. I saw another one begin to wrap itself around his ear.

As fast as I could, I pulled the sticky, wet creatures off me and tossed them over the side of the slow-rolling tram.

Where are they coming from? I wondered.

I glanced up — and a fat, wet one fell over my eyes.

"Yeowwww!" I let out a shriek, grabbed it, flung it away.

The tram turned sharply, sending us both sliding over the seat. The cave narrowed again as we entered a different tunnel. The silvery light glowed dimly around us as we bounced forward.

Two white worms, each at least a foot long, wriggled across my lap. I tugged them off and heaved them over the tram.

Breathing hard, I searched for more. My whole body itched. The back of my neck tingled. I couldn't stop shaking.

"They stopped falling," Marty announced in a shaky voice.

Then why did I still itch?

I rubbed the back of my neck. Stood up and searched the seat, then the floor. I found one last worm, climbing over my shoe. I kicked it away, then dropped back onto the seat with a loud sigh.

"That was totally gross!" I wailed.

Marty scratched his chest, then rubbed his face

with both hands. "I guess that's why they call it The Cave of The Living Creeps," he said. He swept a hand back through his black hair.

I shivered. I couldn't stop itching. I knew the worms were gone, but I could still feel them. "Those disgusting white worms — do you think they were alive?"

Marty shook his head. "Of course not. They were fakes." He snickered. "I guess they fooled you, huh?"

"They sure felt real," I replied. "And the way they wriggled around — "

"They were robots or something," Marty said, scratching his knees. "Everything here is fake. It has to be."

"I'm not so sure," I said, my whole body still itchy and tingling.

"Well, just ask your father," Marty replied grumpily.

I had to laugh. I knew why Marty was suddenly so grouchy. Whether the worms were real or fake, they had scared him. And he knew that I knew that he had been frightened.

"I don't think *little* kids will like the worms," Marty said. "I think they'll get too scared. I'm going to tell that to your dad."

I started to reply — and felt something drop over me. Something scratchy and dry.

It covered my face, my shoulders — my entire body.

I shot both hands up and tried to push it away. It's some kind of a net, I thought.

I grabbed at it, desperate to get it off my face. As I struggled, I turned and saw Marty squirming and batting his arms, caught under the same net.

The tram bounced through the dim cave tunnel. The sticky net felt like cotton candy on my skin.

Marty let out a yelp. "It — it's a big spiderweb!" he stammered.

I tugged and grabbed and pulled. But the sticky threads clung to my face, my arms, and my clothes. "Yuck! This is so gross!" I choked out.

And then I saw the black dots scurrying through the net. It took me a few seconds to realize what they were. Spiders! Hundreds of them!

"Ohhhh." A low moan escaped my throat.

I batted the spiderweb with both hands. I rubbed my cheeks frantically, trying to scrape away the sticky threads. I pulled a spider off my forehead. Another one off the shoulder of my T-shirt.

"The spiders — they're in my hair!" Marty wailed.

He suddenly forgot about acting cool. He began raking his hair with both hands, slapping himself in the head, pinching and swiping at the spiders.

As the tram rolled silently on, we both twisted and squirmed, struggling to flick away the black spiders. I pulled three of them out of my hair. Then I felt one climb into my nose!

I opened my mouth in a horrified scream — and *sneezed* it out.

Marty plucked a spider off my neck and sent it soaring through the air. The last spider. I couldn't see — or feel — any more.

We both dropped down in the seat, breathing hard. My heart pounded in my chest. "Still think everything is a fake?" I asked Marty, my voice weak and small.

"I — I don't know," he replied softly. "The spiders could be puppets maybe. You know. Radio-controlled."

"They were *real!*" I cried sharply. "Face it, Marty — they were real! This is The Cave of The Living Creeps — and they were *living!*"

Marty's eyes grew wide. "You really think so?"

I nodded. "They had to be real spiders."

A smile spread over Marty's face. "That's so *cool!*" he declared. "Real spiders! That is totally cool!"

I let out a long sigh and slumped lower in the seat. I didn't think it was cool at all. I thought it was creepy and disgusting.

These rides are supposed to be *fake*. That's what makes them fun. I decided to tell my dad that the worms and spiders were too scary. He should get rid of them before the studio tour opens to the public.

I crossed my arms in front of me and kept my

eyes straight ahead. I wondered what we would run into next. I hoped there weren't any other disgusting insects waiting to fall on us and climb all over our faces and bodies.

"I think I hear the bats!" Marty teased. He leaned close to me, grinning. "Hear those fluttering sounds? Giant vampire bats!"

I shoved him back to his side of the seat. I wasn't in any mood for his joking around.

"When do we get out of this cave?" I asked impatiently. "This isn't any fun."

"I think it's cool," Marty repeated. "I like exploring caves."

The narrow tunnel opened into a wide cavern. The ceiling appeared to be a mile high. There were giant rocks scattered over the cavern floor. Rocks piled on rocks. Rocks everywhere.

Somewhere ahead of us, I heard water dripping. *Plunk plunk plunk.*

Eerie green light glowed from the cave walls. The tram pulled up to the back wall — and then stopped.

"Now what?" I whispered.

Marty and I turned in our seat, letting our eyes explore the huge cavern. All I could see were rocks. Smooth rocks, some round, some square.

Plunk plunk plunk. Water dripped somewhere to our right. The air felt cold and damp.

"This is kind of boring," Marty murmured. "When do we get going?"

I shrugged. "I don't know. Why did we stop here? It's just a big empty cave."

We waited for the tram to back up and take us out of there.

And waited.

A minute went by. Then another few minutes.

We both turned around and got up on our knees, peering to the back of the tram. Nothing moved. We listened to the steady drip of water, echoing off the high stone walls. No other sound.

Leaning forward against the seatback, I cupped my hands around my mouth and shouted. "Hey — can anybody hear us?"

I waited, listening. No reply.

"Can anybody hear us?" I tried again. "I think we're stuck here!"

No reply. Just the steady *drip drip drip*.

I waited, squinting hard into the glow of green light.

Why wouldn't the tram get moving? Had it broken down? Were we really stuck here?

I turned to Marty. "What's up with this tram? Do you think we're — HEY!"

I gasped as I stared at the empty seat beside me.

I reached both hands out. I grabbed for Marty.

Another lighting trick? Another optical illusion?

"Marty? Hey — Marty?" I croaked.

A cold shiver rolled down my back.

This time Marty was really gone.

52

11

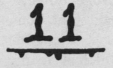

"Marty — ?"

A scraping sound beside the tram made me jump.

I spun around and saw Marty grinning at me from the cave floor. "Gotcha."

"You creep!" I shouted. I swung my fist, but he dodged away, laughing. "*You're* The Living Creep!" I cried. "You deliberately tried to scare me."

"It isn't too hard a job!" he shot back. His smile faded. "I climbed down to check things out."

"But the tram might start up any second!" I told him. "You know what that tour guide told us. She said we should never leave the tram."

Marty squatted down and studied the tires. "I think the tram is stuck or something. Maybe it came off its tracks." He raised his eyes to me and shook his head fretfully. "But there *aren't* any tracks."

"Marty — get back in," I pleaded. "If it starts up and leaves you standing there — "

He grabbed the side of the car with both hands and shook it. The tramcar bounced on its tires. But it didn't move.

"I think it broke down," Marty said softly. "Your father said that some things might not work."

I felt a stab of fear in my chest. "You mean we're *stranded* here? All by ourselves in this creepy cave?"

He stepped to the front of the car and squeezed between the tram and the cave wall. Then he tried to push the tram back, shoving with both hands as hard as he could.

It wouldn't budge.

"Oh, wow," I muttered, shaking my head. "This is horrible. This isn't any fun at all."

I got back up on my knees on the seat and tried shouting again, as loud as I could: "Is anybody in here? Does anybody work here? The tram is stuck!"

Plunk plunk plunk. The dripping water was my only reply.

"Can somebody *help* us?" I shouted. "Please — can somebody help?"

No answer.

"Now what?" I cried.

Marty was still shoving with all his might against the front of the tram. He gave one last hard push, then gave up with a sigh. "You'd better climb down," he said. "We have to walk."

"Huh? Walk? In this creepy dark cave? No way, Marty!"

He came around to my side of the car. "You're not afraid — *are* you, Erin?"

"Yes, I am," I confessed. "A little." I glanced around the huge cavern. "I don't see any exits. We'd have to walk back through those tunnels. With all the spiders and worms and everything."

"We can find a way out," Marty insisted. "There's got to be a door somewhere. They always build emergency exits in these theme park rides."

"I think we should stay in the tram," I said uncertainly. "If we stay here and wait, someone will come and find us."

"It could take days," Marty declared. "Come on, Erin. I'm going to walk. Are you coming with me?"

I shook my head, my arms crossed tightly in front of me. "No way," I insisted. "I'm staying here."

I knew he wouldn't go off by himself. I knew he wouldn't go unless I joined him.

"Well. 'Bye then," he said. He turned and started walking quickly across the cave floor.

"Hey, Marty — ?"

" 'Bye. I'm not waiting here all day. See you later."

He was really leaving. Leaving me alone in the

stalled tram, in the scary cave. "But, Marty —
wait!"

He turned back to me. "Are you coming or not,
Erin?" he called back impatiently.

"Okay, okay," I murmured. I saw that I had no
choice. I climbed over the side of the tram and
dropped to the cave floor.

The dirt was smooth and damp. I started walking slowly toward Marty.

"Hurry it up," he called. "Let's get out of here."
He was walking backward now, motioning for me
to catch up to him.

But I stopped and my mouth dropped open in
horror.

"Don't look at me like that!" he shouted. "Don't
stare at me as if *I'm* doing something wrong!"

But I wasn't staring at Marty.

I was staring at the thing creeping up behind
Marty.

12

"Uh . . . uh . . . uh . . ." I struggled to warn Marty, but only frightened grunts escaped my throat.

He kept backing up, backing right into the enormous creature.

"Erin, get a move on. What's your *problem?*" he demanded.

"Uh . . . uh . . . uh . . ." I finally managed to point.

"Huh?" Marty spun around — and saw it, too. "Whoa!" he screamed. His sneakers slid on the soft cave floor as he came running back to me. "What is *that* thing?"

At first, I thought it was some kind of machine. It looked like one of those tall steel cranes you see on construction sites. All silvery and metallic.

But as it rose up on its wire-thin back legs, I saw that it was *alive!*

It had round black eyes the size of billiard balls. They spun wildly in its skinny silver skull. Two slender antennae bobbed at the top of the head. Its mouth appeared soft, mushy. A gray tongue darted out between long, bristly whiskers.

Its long body stretched back like a folded-up leaf. As it stood, it waved its front legs, short white sticks.

The whole creature looked like some kind of gross stick figure. Its long back legs bent and sprang forward, bent then sprang forward. The thick tongue swung from side to side. The black eyes stopped whirling and focused on me.

"Is it — is it a *grasshopper*?" I choked out.

Marty and I had both backed up to the tram.

Waving its stick arms, the creature sprang closer, its antennae circling slowly on top of its head.

Marty and I pressed our backs against the cold cave wall. We couldn't move back any farther.

"I think it's a praying mantis," Marty replied, staring up at it. The insect had to be at least three times as tall as us. As it moved forward, its head nearly scraped the cave ceiling.

The tongue licked its soft, mushy mouth. The mouth puckered and made loud sucking sounds. My stomach lurched. The sound was so *sick*!

The round black eyes stared down at Marty and me. The giant praying mantis, its body shining like aluminum, took another hopping step toward us. It started to lower its head.

"Wh-what's it going to do?" I stammered, pressing my back hard against the cave wall.

To my surprise, Marty suddenly started to laugh.

I turned to him and grabbed his shoulder. Was he totally losing it?

"Marty — are you okay?"

"Of course!" he replied. He pulled away from me and took a step toward the towering insect. "Why should we be scared, Erin? It's a big robot. It's programmed to walk up to the tram."

"Huh? But, Marty — "

"It's all on a computer," he continued, staring up as the big head bobbed lower on its stick body. "It isn't real. It's part of the ride."

I stared up at the creature. Big drops of saliva rolled off its fat tongue and hit the cave floor with a *splat*.

"It's . . . uh . . . really lifelike," I murmured.

"Your dad is a genius at this stuff!" Marty declared. "We'll have to tell him what a good job he did on the praying mantis." He laughed. "Your dad said there were still some bugs, remember? This must be one of them!"

The insect rubbed its front legs together. It made a shrill whistling sound.

I covered my ears. The high-pitched note made my ears ache!

I was still holding my ears as a second giant

praying mantis hopped out from behind a tall rock.

"Look — another one!" Marty cried, pointing. He tugged my arm. "Wow. They move so smoothly. You can't even tell that they're machines."

The two silvery insects chittered at each other, a sharp shrill, metallic sound. Their black eyes twirled. Their antennae rotated rapidly, excitedly.

Gobs of saliva rolled off their tongues and splattered to the floor. The second one flashed silvery wings on its back, then quickly closed them up again.

"Great-looking robots!" Marty declared. He turned to me. "We'd better get back in the tram. It'll probably start up again now that we've seen these giant bugs."

The two insects chittered to each other. They hopped closer, their sticklike legs springing hard, bouncing off the smooth cave floor.

"I hope you're right," I told Marty. "Those insects are *too* real. I want to get out of here!"

I started to follow him to the tramcar.

The first mantis leaped forward quickly. It hopped between us and the tram, blocking our path.

"Hey — !" I cried.

We tried to step around it. But it took a big hop to stay in front of us.

"It — it won't let us pass!" I stammered.

"Ohhh!" I cried out as the big creature suddenly swung down and slammed its head against my chest. The powerful head-butt sent me sprawling backward.

"Hey — stop that!" I heard Marty shout. "That machine must be broken!"

Its black eyes glowing, the mantis lowered its head again — and gave me another hard push toward the center of the cave.

Its partner moved quickly to trap Marty. It lowered its body and prepared to head-butt Marty. But Marty quickly backed away, raising his hands in front of him like a shield. He hurried to join me.

I heard scraping sounds. Shrill chirps and chittering.

I spun around to discover two more huge, ugly mantises climbing out from behind rocks. Then two more, their antennae twisting excitedly. Their fat gray tongues rolling around their open mouths.

Marty and I huddled together in the middle of the cavern as the creatures hopped and scraped around us. Then they rose up high on their hind legs, their black eyes gleaming, their short stick arms waving.

"We — we're surrounded!" I cried.

13

The giant insects all began chittering at once. They scraped their front legs together excitedly. The shrill whistle rose through the cave, echoing off the stone walls.

They formed a circle around us, leaning back on their spindly hind legs. Moving closer. Tightening the circle. Their tongues whipped back and forth. Thick gobs of mantis saliva hit the floor.

"They're out of control!" Marty shrieked.

"What are they going to do to us?" I cried, covering my ears against their excited chirps and the deafening whistle.

"Maybe they are voice-controlled," Marty shouted. He tilted back his head and shouted up at them: "Stop! Stop!"

They didn't stop.

One of them tilted its silvery head, opened its ugly mouth wide, and spit out a black gob. It splattered onto Marty's sneaker.

He jumped back. His sneaker stuck to the floor.

He struggled to tug it free. "Yuck! Watch out! That black stuff — it's like glue!" he cried.

THOOOM.

Another mantis opened its mouth wide and spit out a big black gob of sticky goo. It splotched the shoulder of my T-shirt.

"Oww!" I wailed. It was so hot — it burned me right through my shirt.

The others chittered shrilly and scraped their hairy stick arms. Their tongues darting back and forth, they began to lower their heads to us.

"The stun guns!" I cried, grabbing Marty's arm. "Maybe the guns will work against these bugs!"

"Those guns are only toys!" he wailed.

THUPPP.

Another black gob missed Marty's foot by inches.

"Besides, the guns are in the tram," Marty continued, staring up at the ugly creatures. "No way they'll let us get to the tram."

"Then what are we going to do?" I cried.

As I asked the question, an idea flashed into my mind.

"Marty — " I whispered. "How do you normally get rid of bugs?"

"Huh? Erin — what are you *talking* about?"

"You step on them — right? Don't you usually step on them?"

"But, Erin — " he protested. "These bugs are big enough to step on *us*!"

"It's worth a try!" I cried.

I raised my sneaker — and tromped as hard as I could on the foot of the nearest mantis.

The giant insect let out a shrill hiss and hopped backward.

Beside me, Marty stomped on another insect, bringing the heel of his sneaker down hard on its spindly foot. That creature fell back, too, raising its head in a shrill hiss of pain. Its eyes spun wildly. Its antennae shot straight up.

I stomped down hard again. With a hoarse choking sound, the big mantis fell onto its side. All four stick legs thrashed the air.

"Let's go!" I shouted.

I turned and burst through the circle of insects. I didn't know where to run. I only knew I had to get away.

The cave erupted in hisses and shrill whistles, angry chittering and croaks. I glimpsed Marty lurching after me.

I ignored the echoing, ringing sounds and ran.

Ran to the tram.

Leaned over the side and grabbed both plastic stun guns into my arms.

Then I pushed away from the tram and hurtled along the stone cave wall.

Where could I go?

How could I escape?

The chittering and hissing grew louder, more frantic. The tall shadows of the giant insects danced on the wall as I ran. I had the feeling that the shadows could reach out and grab me.

I glanced back.

Marty came running behind me at full speed.

The mantises were hopping, scrabbling, limping across the dirt floor after us.

Where to run? Where?

And then I saw the narrow opening in the cave wall. Just a crack, really.

But I dove for it. Slipped into it. Squeezed myself into the dark hole between the stone.

And burst out the other side. Into the misty daylight.

Outside!

I could see trees tilting down the hill. The road that led down to the studio buildings.

Yes! Outside! I made it!

I felt so happy. So *safe*.

But I didn't have long to enjoy the feeling.

As I started to catch my breath, I heard Marty's terrified cry: "Erin — help! Help! They *got* me! They're *eating* me!"

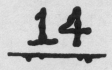

14

With a gasp, I spun around.

How could I help Marty? How could I get him out of the cave?

To my surprise, he was leaning against the cave wall, one elbow against the rock, his legs crossed. A big grin on his round face.

"April Fools," he said.

"YAAAIIIII!" I let out an angry scream. Then I dropped the two plastic pistols and rushed at him, ready to pound him with my fists. "You jerk! You scared me to death!"

He laughed and dodged to the side as I came at him. I swung my fist and hit air.

"Don't play any more dumb jokes like that!" I cried breathlessly. "This place is too scary! Those big insects — "

"Yeah. They were scary," he agreed, his smile fading. "They were so real! How do you think they made them spit like that?"

I shook my head. "I don't know," I muttered.

I had a heavy feeling in my stomach. I knew it was a crazy idea. But I was beginning to think these creatures we were seeing *were* real.

Maybe I've seen too many scary movies. But the big praying mantises and the white worms and all the other creatures and monsters really seemed to be alive.

They didn't move like mechanical creatures. They appeared to breathe. And their eyes focused on Marty and me as if they could really see us.

I wanted to tell Marty what I was thinking. But I knew he would only laugh at me.

He was so sure that they were all robots and that we were seeing some awesome movie special effects. Of course, that made sense. We were on a movie studio tour, after all.

I hoped Marty was right. I hoped it was all tricks. Movie magic.

My dad was a genius when it came to designing mechanical creatures and building theme park rides. And maybe that's all we were seeing. Maybe Dad had really outdone himself this time.

But the heavy feeling in my stomach wouldn't go away. I had the feeling that we were in danger. Real danger.

I had the feeling that something had gone wrong here. That something was out of control.

I suddenly wished we weren't the first two kids

to try out the tour. I knew it was supposed to be a thrill to be the only ones here. But it was too quiet. Too empty. Too scary. It would be so much more fun if hundreds of other people were along with us.

I wanted to tell Marty all this. But how could I?

He was so eager to prove that he was braver than me. So eager to prove that he wasn't afraid of anything.

I couldn't tell him what I was really thinking.

I picked up the two plastic stun guns and handed him one. I didn't want to carry them both.

He tucked the barrel of his gun into his jeans pocket. "Hey, Erin — look where we are!" he cried. He jogged past me, his eyes straight ahead. "Check it out!"

He started running across the grass. I turned and started to follow him. I didn't want him to get too far ahead.

The sky had darkened. The sun had disappeared behind a heavy blanket of clouds. Wisps of gray fog hung low in the cool air. It was nearly evening.

We crossed the road and stepped into a town. I mean, it was a movie set of a town. A small town with low, one- and two-story buildings, small shops, a country-looking general store. Big, old houses in the block beyond the stores.

"Do you think this is a set they really use in the movies?" I asked, hurrying to catch up to Marty.

He turned to me, his dark eyes flashing with excitement. "Don't you recognize it? Don't you know where you are?"

And then my eyes fell on the crumbling, old mansion half-hidden by the twisted trees. And across from it, I saw the crooked picket fence that ran around the old cemetery.

And I knew we were on Shock Street.

"Wow!" I exclaimed, spinning around, trying to take it all in at once. "This really is Shock Street. This is where they filmed all of the movies!"

"It doesn't look the way I imagined it," Marty said. "It looks even scarier!"

He was right. As the sky darkened to evening, long shadows fell over the empty buildings. The wind made a moaning sound as it swept around the corner.

Marty and I made our way down the street, trying to see *everything*. We kept crossing from side to side, peering into a dark, dust-covered shop window — then running to examine the front yard of a rundown, old mansion.

"Check out that empty lot," I said, pointing. "That's where The Mad Mangler hung out. Remember? In *Shocker III?* Remember — he mangled everyone who walked by?"

69

"Of course I remember," Marty snapped. He stepped into the empty lot. Tall weeds bent low, blown by the moaning wind. Shadows moved against the fence at the back.

I stayed on the sidewalk and squinted hard, trying to see what cast the shadows.

Did The Mad Mangler still lurk back there?

The lot was totally empty. So how could there be tall, shifting shadows on the fence?

"Marty — come back," I pleaded. "It's getting dark."

He turned back. "Scared, Erin?"

"It's just an empty lot," I told him. "Let's keep walking."

"People *always* thought it was just an empty lot," Marty replied in a low, scary voice. "Until The Mad Mangler jumped out and mangled them!" He let out a long, evil laugh.

"Marty — you're losing it," I murmured, shaking my head.

He came trotting out of the lot, and we crossed the street. "I wish I had a camera," he said. "I'd really like a picture of me standing in The Mangler's lot." His eyes lit up. "Or even better — !"

He didn't finish his sentence. Instead, he took off, running full speed.

"Hey — wait up!" I cried.

A few seconds later, I saw where he was headed. The old cemetery.

He ran up to the cracked and peeling wooden

gate and turned back to me. "Even better, I'd like a photo of me standing in the cemetery. The actual set where they filmed *Cemetery on Shock Street*."

"We don't have a camera," I called from the street. "Get away from there."

He ignored me and started to open the gate. The bottom was stuck in the grass. Marty tugged hard. Finally, the gate started to pull open, creaking and groaning as it moved.

"Marty — let's go," I insisted. "It's getting late. Dad is probably waiting for us, wondering what happened to us."

"But this is part of the tour!" he insisted. He tugged the heavy gate open just wide enough to squeeze inside the cemetery.

"Marty — please! Don't go in!" I begged. I ran up beside him.

"Erin, it's just a movie set," he replied. "You didn't used to be such a total wimp!"

"I — I just have a bad feeling about this cemetery," I stammered. "A very bad feeling."

"It's part of the tour," he repeated.

"But this gate was *closed*!" I cried. "It was closed so that people don't go in." I raised my eyes to the cemetery. I saw the old graves tilting up from the ground like crooked teeth. "I have such a bad feeling . . ."

Marty ignored me. He tugged the gate open a little wider and slipped into the cemetery.

"Marty — please — !" I gripped the low fence tightly with both hands and watched him.

He took three steps toward the old graves. Then his hands shot straight up in the air — and he dropped out of sight.

15

I stared into the darkness, blinking hard.

I swallowed. Once. Twice.

I couldn't believe that he was gone, that he had vanished so quickly.

The wind moaned between the jagged, tilting gravestones.

"Marty — ?" My voice came out in a choked whisper. "Marty?"

I gripped the picket fence so hard, my hands ached. I knew I had no choice. I had to go in there and see what had happened to him.

I took a deep breath and pushed myself through the opening. The ground was soft. My sneakers sank into the tall grass.

I took one step.

Then another.

I stopped when I heard Marty's voice. "Hey — be careful."

"Huh?" I gazed around. "Where are you?"

"Down here."

I peered down — into a deep, dark hole. An open grave. Marty stared up at me. He had dirt on his cheeks and down the front of his T-shirt. He raised both hands. "Help me out. I fell!"

I had to laugh. He looked ridiculous, standing in that hole, covered in dirt.

"It's not funny. Help me out," he repeated impatiently.

"I warned you," I said. "I had a bad feeling."

"It smells down here," Marty complained.

I leaned down. "What does it smell like?"

"Like dirt. Get me out!"

"Okay, okay." I grabbed his hands and tugged. He kicked his feet, digging his toes of his sneakers into the soft dirt.

A few seconds later, he was back on the ground, frantically brushing himself off. "That was cool!" he declared. "Now I can tell people I was in a grave in The Shock Street Cemetery."

A chill ran down my back as the wind picked up. "Let's get out of here," I pleaded.

Something gray floated silently between two old gravestones. A wisp of fog? A gray cat?

"Check out these graves," Marty said, still brushing dirt off his jeans. "They're all cracked and faded. I can barely read the names. That's so cool. And look how they sprayed cobwebs over that row of stones. Creepy, huh?"

"Marty — can we go?" I begged again. "Dad is

probably worried by now. Maybe the tram started up again. Maybe we can find it."

He ignored me. I watched him lean over a tombstone to read the words cut into it. "Jim Socks," he read. "Eighteen forty to eighteen eighty-seven." He laughed. "Jim Socks. Get it? And look at the ones next to it. Ben Dover. Sid Upp. These are all funny!"

I laughed. Ben Dover and Sid Upp were pretty funny.

My laugh was cut short when I heard a soft cry from the back of the graveyard. I saw another gray wisp dart behind a tombstone.

I held my breath and listened hard. The wind whistled through the tall grass.

Rising above the wind came another shrill cry.

A cat? I wondered. Is the cemetery filled with cats? Or is it a child?

Marty heard it, too. He moved down the row of stones until he stood beside me. His dark eyes glowed excitedly. "This is so cool. Did you hear the sound effects? There must be a speaker hidden in the ground."

Another shrill cry.

Definitely human. A girl?

I shivered. "Marty, I really think we should try to get back to my dad. We've been here all afternoon. And — "

"But what about the rest of the tour?" he argued. "We have to see everything!"

I heard another cry. Louder. Closer. A cry of terror.

I tried to ignore it. Marty was probably right. The cries had to be coming from a loudspeaker somewhere.

"How can we finish the tour?" I demanded. "We were supposed to stay on the tram — remember? But the tram — OHH!"

I cried out as a hand shot up from the ground in front of us. A green hand. Its long fingers unfolded, as if reaching for us.

"Whoa!" Marty cried, stumbling back.

Another green hand shot up from the dirt. Then two more.

Hands reaching up from graves.

I let out a frightened gasp. Hands were bursting up through the grass. Hands all around us. Their fingers twisting and arching, reaching out.

Marty started to laugh. "This is totally awesome! Just like in the movie!"

He stopped laughing as a hand poked up beside him and grabbed his ankle. "Erin — help!" he cried.

But I couldn't help.

Two green hands had wrapped around my ankles and were pulling me down, down into the grave.

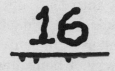

16

"Come dowwwwwnnnnn," a soft voice moaned. *"Come dowwwwwnnnn with us."*

"Nooo!" I shrieked.

My arms thrashed the air. I tried to kick, but the hands gripped me so tightly, so firmly.

My whole body frantically jerked and tilted back and forth, as I struggled not to fall. If I fell, I knew they would grab my hands, too. And pull me facedown into the earth.

"Come dowwwwwwwwnnnnnnn. Come dowww-wwnnnn with us."

This isn't a joke, I thought. These hands are *real.* They are really trying to pull me underground.

"Help! Oh, help!" I heard Marty's cry. Then I saw him fall. He toppled to the grass, onto his knees.

Two hands gripped his ankles. Two more green hands poked up from the dirt to grab his wrists.

"Come dowwwwwwwnnnnnnn. Come dowww-wwnnnn with us," the sad voice moaned.

"Noooo!" I shrieked, tugging wildly, desperately.

To my surprise, I pulled free.

One foot sank into the soft grass. I glanced down. My sneaker had slid off. The hand still gripped the sneaker — but my foot was free.

With a happy cry, I bent down. Pulled off the other sneaker.

I was free now. Free!

Breathing hard, I bent and quickly pulled off my socks. I knew it would be easier to run barefoot. I tossed the socks away. Then I hurried over to Marty.

He was flat on his stomach. Six hands held him down, tugging at him, tugging hard. His whole body twisted and shook.

He raised his head when he saw me. "Erin — help me!" he gasped.

I dropped to my knees. Reached for his sneakers. Tugged them off.

The green hands gripped the sneakers tightly. Marty kicked his feet free and tried to climb to his knees.

I grabbed a green hand and pulled if off his wrist. The hand slapped at me. A cold, hard slap that made my hand ring with pain.

Ignoring it, I grabbed for another green hand.

Marty rolled over. Rolled free. Jumped to his

feet, gasping, trembling, his mouth hanging open, his dark eyes bulging.

"Your socks — " I cried breathlessly. "Pull them off! Hurry!"

He clumsily tore them off his feet.

The hands grabbed wildly for us. Dozens of hands stretching up from the dirt. Hundred of hands reaching up for us from the tall graveyard grass.

"Come dowwwwwwwnnnnnnn. Come dowww-wwnnnn with us," the voice moaned.

"Come dowwwwwwwnnnnnnn. Come dowww-wwnnnn," a dozen other soft voices called from beneath the ground.

Marty and I froze. The soft, sad voices seemed to hypnotize me. My legs suddenly felt as if they were made of stone.

"Come dowwwwwwwnnnnnnn. Come dowww-wwnnnn."

And then I saw a green head pop up from the dirt. And then another head. Another. Bald green heads with empty eye sockets and open, toothless mouths.

I saw shoulders, then arms. More heads poking up. Bright-green bodies pulling up from beneath the ground.

"M-Marty — " I choked out. "They're coming up after us!"

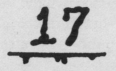

17

The cemetery rang out with grunts and groans as the ugly green figures pulled themselves up from the ground.

I took one last glance at their tattered, shredded clothing, at their blackened eye sockets, their toothless, grinning mouths.

And then I started to run.

Marty and I both ran without saying a word. Side by side, we darted across the tall grass between the rows of crooked tombstones.

My heart thudded in my chest. My head throbbed. My bare feet sank into the cold dirt, slipped on the tall, damp grass.

Marty reached the wooden gate first. He was running so hard, he banged into the fence. He let out a cry — then slipped through the gate onto Shock Street.

I could hear moans and groans and eerie calls of the disgusting green people behind me. But I didn't look back. I dove for the gate. Squeezed through. Then I shoved it shut behind me.

Running into the street, I stopped to catch my breath. I bent over and pressed my hands against my knees. My side ached. I sucked in breath after breath.

"Don't stop!" Marty cried frantically. "Erin — keep going!"

I took a deep breath and followed him down the street. Our bare feet slapped the pavement.

I could still hear the moans and calls behind us. But I was too scared to glance back.

"Marty — where *is* everybody?" I called breathlessly.

Shock Street was empty, the houses and shops all dark.

Shouldn't there be people around? I wondered. This is a big movie studio. Where are the people who work for Shocker Studios? Where are the people who work on the studio tour?

Why isn't anyone around to help us?

"Something is wrong!" Marty choked out, running at full speed. We passed The Horror Hardware Store and Shock City Electronics. "The robots are out of control or something!"

At last! Marty agreed with me. He finally agreed that something was terribly wrong.

"We've got to find your dad," Marty said, running across the street to the next block of dark houses. "We've got to tell him there's a problem."

"We have to find the tram," I called, struggling to keep up with him. "Ow!"

My bare foot came down on something hard. A rock or something. Pain shot up my leg. But I hobbled on.

"If we can get back on the tram, it will take us back to Dad," I called.

"There *has* to be a way out of Shock Street," Marty said. "It's only a movie set."

We ran past a tall mansion with two turrets. It looked like an evil castle. I didn't remember it from any of the *Shocker* movies.

Beyond the mansion stretched a big, empty dirt lot. At the back of the lot stood a low brick wall, just a foot or two taller than Marty and me.

"Cut through here!" I told Marty. "If we can climb up on that wall, we can probably see the studio road."

I was just guessing. But it was worth a try.

We both turned into the empty lot.

My bare feet thudded over the soft dirt.

The dirt felt cold and wet. As we crossed the field, our feet tossed up big clumps of mud.

I pumped my legs harder as the mud grew softer. My bare feet were sinking into it. As I ran, the cold mud rose up over my ankles.

Marty and I were nearly to the brick wall when we ran into the sinkhole.

"Yaaaaaiiii!" We both uttered hoarse cries as the ground gave way beneath us.

The mud made a sick *splussssh* as we sank.

I tossed up both hands. Tried to grab onto something.

But there was nothing to grab.

The mud oozed around me. Over my ankles. My legs. Up over my knees.

It's sucking me down, I thought. I tried to cry out again — but panic choked my throat.

I glimpsed Marty beside me. His arms were waving wildly. His whole body twisted and squirmed as he sank. The mud was up over his waist — and he was still sinking fast.

I kicked hard. Tried to raise my knees.

But I was trapped. Trapped and dropping down, down into the dark, wet ooze.

My mud-covered arms slapped against the surface.

I couldn't stop myself.

The mud bubbled up over my neck. And I was sinking fast.

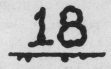

18

I held my breath. The mud rose up to my chin.

In a second, it will be over my head, I thought.

A sob escaped my throat.

The mud crept higher, up over my chin. I started to spit as it reached my mouth.

And then I felt something grab my arm. Strong hands slipped under my arms. I felt the hands slide in the mud.

They gripped me harder.

I felt myself being tugged up, tugged by someone very strong.

The mud made a loud *plop* as I rose up. I felt the mud roll down my chest, my legs, my knees.

And then I was standing on the surface, still held by the two powerful hands.

"Marty — !" I called, tasting the sour mud on my lips. "Are you — ?"

"I'm up!" I heard his hoarse reply. "Erin, I'm okay!"

The strong hands finally let go. My legs trembled. I wobbled but remained standing.

I turned to see who had rescued me.

And stared into the glowing red eyes of a wolf.

A human with the face of a wolf. Clawed hands covered in black fur. A long, brown snout curved in an open, toothy grin. Sharp, pointed ears above a thick tuft of black wolf fur.

A female. She wore a silvery catsuit. Sleek and tight-fitting. As I stared in shock, she opened her mouth in a throaty growl.

I recognized her at once. Wolf Girl!

I turned to see her companion — Wolf Boy. He had pulled Marty out of the mud hole. Marty's whole body was caked in mud. He tried to wipe his face, but only managed to smear more mud over his cheeks.

"You — saved us! Thank you!" I cried, finally finding my voice.

The two werewolves uttered low growls in reply.

"We — we lost the tram," I explained to Wolf Girl. "We need to get back. You know. Back to where the ride began."

She let out a sharp growl. Then she snapped her toothy jaw hard.

"Please — " I begged. "Can you help us get back to the tram? Or can you take us to the main building? My dad is waiting for me there."

Wolf Girl's red eyes flashed. She growled again.

"We know you're just actors!" Marty blurted out shrilly. "But we don't want to be scared anymore. We've had enough scares for today. Okay?"

The two werewolves growled. A long white string of saliva drooled over Wolf Boy's black lips.

Something inside me snapped. I totally lost it. "Stop it!" I screamed. "Just stop it! Marty is right! We don't want to be scared now. So stop the werewolf act — and help us!"

The werewolves growled again. Wolf Girl snapped her jaws. A long pink tongue slid out, and she licked her jagged teeth hungrily.

"That's *enough!*" I shrieked. "Stop the act! Stop it! Stop it!"

I was so angry, so *furious* — I reached up with both hands. I grabbed the fur on the sides of Wolf Girl's mask.

And I tugged the mask with all my strength.

Tugged. Tugged with both hands as hard as I could.

And felt real fur. And warm skin.

It wasn't a mask.

19

"Ohh." I let out a gasp, and jerked my hands away.

The werewolf's red eyes glowed. Her black lips parted. Once again, her tongue flicked hungrily over her yellow, pointed teeth.

My whole body trembled as I backed up against the brick wall. "M-Marty — " I stammered. "It's not an act."

"Huh?" Marty stood stiffly in front of Wolf Boy, his dark eyes wide in his mud-caked face.

"They're not actors," I whispered. "Something is wrong here. Something is terribly wrong."

Marty's mouth dropped open. He took a step back.

Both werewolves uttered low growls. They lowered their heads as if preparing to attack.

"Do you believe me?" I cried. "Do you finally believe me?"

Marty nodded. He didn't say a word. I think he was too terrified to talk.

Saliva poured from the werewolves' mouths. Their eyes glowed like fire in the darkness. Their furry chests began to heave in and out. Their breaths came loud and hoarse.

I jumped back against the wall as both werewolves raised their heads and let out long, frightening howls.

What were they going to do to us?

I grabbed Marty and tugged him to the wall. "Up!" I cried. "Get up! Maybe they can't reach us up there!"

Marty leaped high, stretching up his arms. His hands slapped the top of the wall, then slid back down. He tried again. He bent his knees. Jumped. Grabbed for the top of the wall. Slipped back down.

"I can't!" he wailed. "It's too high."

"We've got to!" I shrieked.

I turned back and saw the two werewolves lean back on their hind legs and then spring up. They were snarling and growling now, thick gobs of saliva running over their snapping teeth.

"Up!" I cried.

As Marty leaped for the wall again, I reached down and grabbed his muddy foot. "Up!" I gave him a hard boost.

His hands thrashed the air. Caught the top of the brick wall. Held on.

His bare feet kicked the air. But he held on and tugged himself up.

On his knees on top of the wall, he turned and grabbed my hands. He pulled and I jumped. I struggled to scramble up beside him.

But I couldn't get my knees up. Couldn't get them onto the wall.

My bare feet thrashed wildly. My knees scraped against the wall as Marty tugged.

"I can't do it! I can't!" I gasped.

The werewolves howled again.

"Keep trying!" Marty choked out. He tugged my arms. Tugged with all his strength.

I was still struggling as the two werewolves leaped.

20

I heard the snap of jaws.

I felt hot breath on the bottom of my foot.

The two werewolves thudded against the wall.

With a desperate cry, I sprang to the top. Gasping for air, I pressed myself flat against the bricks.

I raised my head in time to see the two snarling werewolves leap again. Jaws snapped in front of my face. Red eyes gleamed hungrily at me.

"No!" With a cry, I scrambled to my feet.

The werewolves raised their heads in angry howls and prepared to attack again.

Marty and I stood pressed close together, staring down at them.

They jumped.

Their claws scraped against the bricks. The shrill screech sent chills down my back. Their teeth snapped.

They dropped down. Prepared another leap, snarling excitedly.

"We can't stay up here forever!" Marty cried. "What do we do?"

I squinted into the darkness. Was that the studio road on the other side of the wall?

Too dark to tell.

The werewolves leaped again. Jagged teeth scraped against my ankle.

I jumped back. Nearly toppled off the wall.

Marty and I bumped into each other, our eyes on the two growling creatures preparing another leap.

The gun! The plastic stun gun!

Mine had fallen from my hand. It was probably buried in that mud hole. But my eyes fell on Marty's gun. Its handle poked out from his jeans pocket.

Without saying a word, I grabbed the handle and tugged the plastic pistol from Marty's jeans.

"Hey — !" he cried. "Erin — what are you doing?"

"They gave us the guns for a reason," I explained, shouting over the frightening howls of the two werewolves. "Maybe this will stop them."

"It — it's only a *toy*!" Marty stammered.

I didn't care. It was worth a try.

Maybe it would frighten them. Maybe it would hurt them. Maybe it would chase them away.

I raised the plastic gun. Aimed it as the two werewolves made another leap of attack.

"One — two — three — FIRE!"

I squeezed the trigger. Again. Again.

Again!

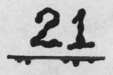

The gun made a loud buzzing sound. It shot out a beam of yellow light.

Yes! I thought. Yes! I prayed.

The light will stop them.

It's a stun gun — right? The buzzing sound and the bright light will stun them. It will freeze them in place so Marty and I can make our escape.

I squeezed the trigger hard. Again. Again.

It didn't stop the werewolves. It didn't even seem to surprise them.

They leaped higher. I felt sharp claws scrape my leg. I cried out in pain.

And the plastic gun flew out of my hand.

It clattered against the top of the wall, then slid to the ground.

Just a toy. Marty was right. It wasn't a real weapon. It was just a stupid toy.

"Look out!" Marty opened his mouth in a shrill shriek as the snarling creatures made another high leap at the wall.

Claws scraped the brick — and held on. Red eyes glared up at me. Hot wolf breath tingled my skin.

"Ohhh." My arms flew up as I lost my balance. I struggled to stay up. But my knees bent. My feet slipped.

I grabbed for Marty. Missed.

And toppled off. Landed hard on my back on the other side of the wall.

Gazing up in horror, I saw Marty leap down beside me.

The two werewolves were on the top of the wall now. They glared down at us, red eyes glowing, tongues out, breathing hard.

Preparing to pounce.

Marty dragged me to my feet. "Run!" he cried hoarsely, his eyes wide with panic.

The werewolves growled above us.

The ground tilted. I still felt dizzy, a little dazed from my fall. "We — we can't outrun them!" I moaned.

I heard a rumbling sound. A clatter.

Marty and I both turned. And saw two yellow eyes, glowing against the dark sky.

Yellow eyes of a creature roaring toward us.

No. Not a creature.

As it drew nearer, I could make out its long, sleek shape.

The tram!

The tram bouncing over the road behind yellow headlights. Coming closer. Closer.

Yes!

I turned to Marty. Did he see it, too? He did.

Without saying a word, we both began running to the road. The tram was rolling fast. Somehow we had to climb on it. We *had* to!

Behind us, I heard the werewolves howl. I heard a hard *thump*, then another as they dropped off the wall.

The twin yellow headlights of the tram swept over us.

The werewolves snarled and howled angrily as they chased after us.

A few feet ahead of me, Marty was hurtling forward, his head down, his legs pumping furiously.

The tram bumped closer. Closer.

The howling werewolves were inches behind us. I could almost feel their hot breath on the back of my neck.

A few more seconds. A few more seconds — and Marty and I would make our jump.

I watched the tram speed around a curve, the yellow headlights washing over the dark road. I kept my eyes on the front car. Took a deep breath. Prepared to jump.

And then Marty fell.

I saw his hands shoot out. Saw his mouth open wide in surprise. In horror.

He stumbled over his own bare feet and dropped to the ground, landing hard on his stomach.

I couldn't stop in time.

I ran right into him. Stumbled over him.

Fell heavily on top of him.

And watched the tram speed past us.

22

"Owoooooooo!"

The two werewolves uttered long howls of triumph.

My heart pounding, I scrambled to my feet. "Get up!" I frantically pulled Marty up by both arms.

We took off after the tram, our bare feet pounding the hard road. The last car bounced a few feet ahead of us.

I reached it first. Shot out my right hand. Grabbed the back of the car.

With a desperate leap, I hoisted myself up. Up. And into the last seat.

Struggling to catch my breath, I turned back to find Marty running behind the tram. His hands reached for the back of the tramcar. "I — I can't make it!" he gasped.

"Run! You've *got* to!" I screamed.

Behind him, I could see the werewolves scampering close behind.

Marty put on a burst of speed. He grabbed the back of the car with both hands. It dragged him for several feet — until he swung himself around and dropped into the seat beside me.

Yes! I thought happily. We made it! We got away from those howling werewolves.

Or did we?

Would they jump into the tram after us?

I spun around, my whole body trembling. And I watched the werewolves fade into the distance. They ran for a while, then gave up. They both stood in the road, hunched over in defeat, watching us escape.

Escape.

What a wonderful word.

Marty and I grinned at each other. I slapped him a high five.

We were both breathing hard, covered in mud. My legs ached from running. My bare feet throbbed. My heart still thudded from the frightening chase.

But we had escaped. And now we were safe in the tram, on our way back to the starting platform. Back to my dad.

"We've got to tell your dad that this place is messed up," Marty said breathlessly.

"Something is horribly wrong here," I agreed.

"Those werewolves — they weren't kidding around," Marty continued. "They — they were real, Erin. They weren't actors."

I nodded. I felt so glad that Marty finally agreed with me. And he wasn't pretending to be brave anymore. He wasn't pretending that it was all robots and special effects.

We both knew that we had faced *real* dangers. *Real* monsters.

Something was terribly wrong at Shocker Studios. Dad had told us he wanted a full report. Well, he was going to get one!

I settled back in the seat, trying to calm down.

But I shot straight up again when I realized we weren't alone. "Marty — look!" I pointed to the front of the tram. "We aren't the only passengers."

In fact, every tramcar appeared to be filled with people.

"What's going on?" Marty murmured. "Your dad said we were the only ones on the tour. And now the tram is — OH! — "

Marty never finished his sentence. His mouth fell open in a gasp. His eyes bulged open wide.

I gasped, too.

The other passengers on the tram all turned around at the same time. And I saw their grinning jaws, their dark, empty eye sockets, the gray bones of their skulls.

Skeletons.

The other passengers were all grinning skeletons.

Their jaws opened in dry laughter. Cruel laughter that sounded like the wind screeching through bare trees. Bones rattled and clattered as they raised their yellowed, skeletal hands to point at us.

Their skulls bobbed and bounced as the tram carried us, faster, faster, through the darkness.

Marty and I slumped low in the seat, trembling, staring at the grinning skulls, the pointing fingers.

Who *were* they?

How did they get on this tram?

Where were they taking us?

23

The skeletons laughed their wheezing laugh. Their bones clanked and rattled. Their yellowed skulls bounced loosely on their clattering shoulder bones.

The tram picked up speed. We were flying through the darkness.

I forced myself to turn away from the grinning skulls and peered out. Beyond the trees, I could see the low buildings of the movie studio. As I stared, they grew smaller, faded into the blackness of the night.

"Marty — we're not going back to the main platform," I whispered. "We're heading the wrong way. We're going *away* from all the buildings."

He swallowed hard. I could see the panic in his eyes. "What can we do?" he choked out.

"We've got to get off!" I replied. "We've got to jump."

Marty had slumped all the way down in the seat,

as low as he could get. I think he was trying to hide from the skeletons.

Now he raised his head and peeked over the side of the tram. "Erin — we can't jump!" he cried. "We're going too fast."

He was right.

We were rocketing along the road. And the tram kept picking up speed. The trees and shrubs whirred past in a dark blur.

And then as we squealed into a sharp curve, a tall building seemed to jump into our path.

A castle, bathed in swirling spotlights. All gray and silver. Twin towers reached up to the sky. A solid stone wall rose up from the road.

The road.

It curved straight into the castle wall. The road ended at the wall.

And we were roaring down the road, still picking up speed.

Roaring toward the castle.

The skeletons rattled and clattered and laughed their dry, screeching laugh. They bounced in their seats, bones cracking, jumping in excitement as we zoomed at the castle.

Closer. Closer.

Right up to it now. Up to the solid stone wall.

About to smash right into it.

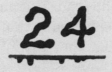

24

My legs trembled. My heart pounded. But somehow I managed to stand up on the seat.

I took a deep breath. Held it. Closed my eyes — and jumped.

I landed hard on my side, and rolled.

I saw Marty hesitate. The tram bounced. Marty dove over the side.

He hit the ground on his stomach. Rolled onto his back. And kept rolling.

I came to a stop under a tree. And turned to the castle — in time to see the tram plunge into the stone wall.

Without a sound.

The first tramcar hit the castle wall and flew through it.

Silently.

I could see the skeletons bobbing and bouncing.

And I saw the next car and the next and the next — all shoot into the castle wall and disappear through it without making a sound.

A few seconds later, the tram disappeared.

A heavy silence fell over the road

The spotlights on the castle wall dimmed.

"Erin — are you okay?" Marty called weakly.

I turned to find him on his hands and knees on the other side of the road. I scrambled to my feet. I had scraped my side, but it didn't hurt too badly.

"I'm okay," I told him. I pointed to the castle. "Did you see that?"

"I saw it," Marty replied, standing up slowly. "But I don't believe it." He stretched. "How did the tram go through the wall? Do you think the castle isn't really there? That it's an optical illusion? Some kind of trick?"

"There's an easy way to find out," I said.

We walked side by side on the road. The wind rustled the trees, making them whisper all around us. The pavement felt cold under my bare feet.

"We've got to find my dad," I said quietly. "I'm sure he can explain everything to us."

"I hope so," Marty murmured.

We stepped up to the castle wall. I stuck out both hands, expecting them to go right through.

But my hands slapped solid stone.

Marty lowered his shoulder and shoved it against the castle wall. His shoulder hit the wall with a *thud*.

"It's solid," Marty said, shaking his head. "It's a real wall. So how did the tram go through it?"

"It's a ghost tram," I whispered, rubbing my

hand against the cold stone. "A ghost tram filled with skeletons."

"But we *rode* in it!" Marty cried.

I slapped the wall with both hands and spun away from it. "I'm sick of mysteries!" I wailed. "I'm sick of being scared! I'm sick of werewolves and monsters! I'm never going to another scary movie as long as I live!"

"Your father can explain it all," Marty said softly, shaking his head. "I'm sure he can."

"I don't want him to explain it!" I cried. "I just want to get *away* from here!"

Keeping close together, we made our way around to the side of the castle. I could hear strange, animal howls behind us. And a frightening cackle cut through the air somewhere above our heads.

I ignored all the sounds. I didn't want to think about whether they were being made by real monsters or fakes. I didn't want to think about the frightening creatures we had run into — or the close calls Marty and I had had.

I didn't want to think.

At the back of the castle, the road appeared again. "I hope we're going in the right direction," I murmured, following it as it curved into the hill.

"Me, too," Marty replied in a tiny voice.

We picked up our pace, walking quickly in the middle of the road. We tried not to pay attention to the sharp animal calls, the shrill cries, the howls and moans that seemed to follow us everywhere.

The road sloped uphill. Marty and I leaned forward as we climbed. The frightening cries and howls followed us up the hill.

As we neared the top, I saw several low buildings.

"Yes!" I cried. "Marty — look! We must be heading back to the main platform." I started jogging toward the buildings. Marty trotted close behind.

We both stopped when we realized where we were.

Back on Shock Street.

Somehow we had made a circle.

Past the old houses and small shops, The Shock Street Cemetery came into view. Staring at the fence, I remembered the green hands poking up from the ground. The green shoulders. The green faces. The hands pulling us, pulling us down.

My whole body shuddered.

I didn't want to be back here. I never wanted to see this terrifying street again.

But I couldn't turn away from the cemetery. As I stared at the old gravestones from across the street, I saw something move.

A wisp of gray. Like a tiny cloud.

It rose up between two crooked, old stones. Floated silently into the air.

And then another puff of gray lifted off the ground. And another.

I glimpsed Marty. He stood beside me, hands pressed against his waist, staring hard. He saw them, too.

The gray puffs rose silently, like snowballs or cotton. Dozens of them, floating up from the graves.

Floating over the cemetery and out over the street.

Floating above Marty and me. Hovering so low.

And then as we stared up at them, they started to grow. To inflate, like gray balloons.

And I saw faces inside them. Dark faces, etched in shadow like the Man in the Moon. The faces scowled at us. Old faces, lined and creased. Eyes narrowed to dark slits. Frowning faces. Sneering faces inside the billowing, white puffs.

I grabbed Marty's shoulder. I wanted to run, to get away, to get out from under them.

But, like smoke, the wisps of mist with their evil faces, swirled down, swirled around us. Trapped us. Trapped us inside.

The faces, the ugly, scowling faces, spinning around us. Spinning faster, faster, holding us in the swirling, choking mist.

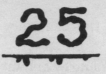

I pressed my hands over my eyes, trying to shut them out.

I froze in total panic. I couldn't think. I couldn't breathe.

I could hear the shrill rush of wind as the ghostly clouds swirled around us.

And then I heard a man's voice, shouting over the wind: "Cut! Print that one! Good scene, everyone!"

I lowered my hands slowly and opened my eyes. I let out my breath in a long whoosh.

A man came striding up to Marty and me. He wore jeans and a gray sweatshirt under a brown leather jacket. He had a blue-and-white Dodgers cap sideways on his head. A blond ponytail tumbled out from under it.

He carried a clipboard in one hand. He had a silver whistle around his neck. He smiled at Marty and me and flashed us a thumbs-up.

"Hey, what's up, guys? I'm Russ Denver. Good job! You looked really scared."

"Huh?" I cried, my mouth dropping open. "We *were* really scared!"

"I'm so glad to see a real live human!" Marty cried.

"This tour — it's totally messed up!" I shrieked. "The creatures — they're alive! They tried to hurt us! They really did! It wasn't any fun! It wasn't like a ride!" The words spilled out of me in a rush.

"It was really gross! The werewolves snapped at us and chased us up a wall!" Marty exclaimed.

The two of us started talking at once, telling this guy Denver all of the frightening things that had happened to us on the tour.

"Whoa! Whoa!" A smile crossed his handsome face. He raised his clipboard as if to shield himself from us. "It's all special effects, guys. Didn't they explain to you that we're making a movie here? That we were filming your reactions?"

"No. No one explained that, Mr. Denver!" I replied angrily. "My dad brought us here. He designed the studio tour. And he told us we were the first to try it out. But he didn't tell us about any movie being filmed. I really think — "

I felt Marty's hand on my shoulder. I knew Marty was trying to calm me down. But I didn't *want* to be calmed down.

I was really angry.

Mr. Denver turned back to a group of crew members behind him in the street. "Take thirty, guys. Let's break for dinner."

They moved away, talking among themselves. Mr. Denver turned back to us. "Your father should have explained to you — "

"It's okay. Really," Marty interrupted. "We just got a little scared. All of the creatures seemed so real. And we didn't see any other people anywhere. You're the first real person we've seen all afternoon."

"My dad must be really worried," I told the movie director. "He said he'd be waiting for us on the main platform. Can you tell us how to get there?"

"No problem," Mr. Denver replied. "See that big house there with the open door?" He pointed with his clipboard.

Marty and I stared at the house across the street. A narrow path led up to the house. A pale yellow light shone inside the open front door.

"That's Shockro's House of Shocks," the director explained. "Go right in that door and straight through the house."

"But won't we get shocked in there?" Marty demanded. "In the movie, anyone who goes into Shockro's house gets jolted with twenty million volts of electricity!"

"That's just in the movie," Mr. Denver replied.

110

"The house is just a set. It's perfectly safe. Go through the house. Then out the back, and you will see the main building on the other side of the street. You can't miss it."

"Thank you!" Marty and I called out at once.

Marty turned and started running full speed toward the house.

I turned back to Mr. Denver. "I'm sorry for yelling before," I told him. "I was just so scared, and I thought — "

I gasped.

Mr. Denver had turned away. And I saw the long power cord — the power cord that was plugged into his back.

He wasn't a real human. He wasn't a movie director. He was some kind of robot.

He was fake like all the others. He was lying to us. Lying!

I turned and cupped my hands around my mouth. I started to run, frantically calling after Marty: "Don't go in there! Marty — stop! Don't go in that house!"

Too late.

Marty was already running through the door.

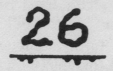

26

"Marty — wait! Stop!" I shouted as I ran.

I had to stop him.

The director was a fake. I knew he wasn't telling the truth.

"Marty — *please!*"

My bare feet pounded the hard pavement. I plunged up the path as Marty trotted into the doorway.

"Stop!"

I flew to the doorway. Reached out both hands. Made a wild dive to tackle him.

And missed.

I skidded across the walk on my stomach.

As soon as Marty entered the house, I saw the flash of white light. I heard a loud buzz. Then the sharp crackle of electricity.

The room exploded in a flash of lightning. So bright I had to shield my eyes.

When I opened them, I saw Marty sprawled

facedown on the floor. "Nooooo!" I let out a terrified wail.

Scrambling to my feet, I dove into the house.

Would I get shocked, too?

I didn't care. I had to get to Marty. I had to help him out of there.

"Marty! Marty!" I screamed his name again and again.

He didn't move.

"Marty — please!" I grabbed his shoulders and started to shake him. "Wake up, Marty! Snap out of it! Marty!"

He didn't open his eyes.

I suddenly felt a chill. A dark shadow slid over me.

And I realized I wasn't alone in the house.

27

I spun around with a gasp.

Was it Shockro? Some other scary creature?

A tall figure leaned over me. I squinted into the darkness, struggling to see his face.

"Dad!" I cried as he came into focus. "Dad! Oh, I'm so glad to see you!"

"Erin, what are you doing here?" he asked in a low voice.

"It — it's Marty!" I stammered. "You've got to help him, Dad. He's been shocked and he — he — "

Dad leaned closer. Behind his eyeglasses, his brown eyes were cold. His face set in a troubled frown.

"*Do* something, Dad!" I pleaded. "Marty is hurt. He isn't moving. He won't open his eyes. The studio tour was so *awful*, Dad! Something is wrong. Something is *terribly* wrong!"

He didn't reply. He leaned closer.

And as his face came into the soft light, I saw that he wasn't my father!

"Who *are* you?" I shrieked. "You're not my dad! Why aren't you helping me? Why aren't you helping Marty? Do something — please! Where's my dad? Where *is* he? Who *are* you? Help me! Somebody? Help me AAAAAARRRRRRRR. Help MRRRRRRRRRRR. Dad — MARRRRRRR-RRRRRR. DRRRMMMMMMMMmmmmm."

28

Mr. Wright stood staring down at Erin and Marty. He shook his head unhappily. He shut his eyes and let out a long sigh.

Jared Curtis, one of the studio engineers, came running into The House of Shocks. "Mr. Wright, what happened to your two kid robots?" he demanded.

Mr. Wright sighed again. "Programming problems," he muttered.

He pointed to the Erin robot, frozen in place on her knees beside the Marty robot. "I had to shut the girl off. Her memory chip must be bad. The Erin robot was supposed to think of me as her father. But just now, she didn't recognize me."

"And what about the Marty robot?" Jared asked.

"It's totally down," Mr. Wright replied. "I think the electrical system shorted out."

"What a shame," Jared said, bending to roll the Marty robot over. He pulled up. the T-shirt and fiddled with some dials on the back. "Hey, Mr. Wright, it was a great idea to make robot kids to test the park. I think we can fix them."

Jared opened up a panel on Marty's back and squinted at the red and green wires. "All the other creatures, and monsters, and robots worked perfectly. Not a single bug."

"I should have known there was a problem yesterday," Mr. Wright said. "We were in my office. The Erin robot asked about her mother. I built her. She doesn't have a mother."

Mr. Wright tossed up his hands. "Oh, well. No problem. We'll reprogram these two. Put in new chips. They'll be good as new in no time. Then we'll try them out once again on the Shocker Studio Tour, before we open the park to real kids."

He took the Marty robot from Jared and slung it over his shoulder. Then he picked up the Erin robot. He tossed it over his other shoulder. Then, humming to himself, he carried them to the engineering building.

Add *more*

to your collection . . .

Here's a chilling preview of

EGG MONSTERS FROM MARS

1

Three girls from Brandy's class came running across the lawn. I recognized them. They were the girls I call the Hair Sisters. They're not sisters. But they spend all their time in Brandy's room after school doing each other's hair.

Dad moved slowly across the grass toward them. He had his camcorder up to his face. The three Hair Sisters waved to the camera and yelled, "Happy Birthday, Brandy!"

Dad tapes all our birthdays and vacations and big events. He keeps the tapes on a shelf in the den. We never watch them.

The sun beamed down. The grass smelled sweet and fresh. The spring leaves on the trees were just starting to unfurl.

"Okay — everyone follow me to the back!" Brandy ordered.

The kids lined up in twos and threes, carrying

their baskets. Anne and I followed behind them. Dad walked backwards, busily taping everything.

Brandy led the way to the backyard. Mom was waiting there. "The eggs were hidden everywhere," Mom announced, sweeping her hand in the air. "Everywhere you can imagine."

"Okay, everyone!" Brandy cried. "At the count of three, the egg hunt begins! *One* —"

Anne leaned down and whispered in my ear. "Bet you five dollars I collect more eggs than you."

I smiled. Anne always knows how to make things more interesting.

"*Two* —"

"You've got a bet!" I told her.

"*Three!*" Brandy called.

The kids all cheered. The hunt for hidden eggs was on.

They all began hurrying through the backyard, bending down to pick up eggs. Some of them moved on hands and knees through the grass. Some worked in groups. Some searched through the yard on their own.

I turned and saw Anne stooping down, moving quickly along the side of the garage. She already had three eggs in her basket.

I can't let her win! I told myself. I sprang into action.

I ran past a cluster of girls around the old doghouse. And I kept moving.

I wanted to find an area of my own. A place where I could grab up a bunch of eggs without having to compete with the others.

I jogged across the tall grass, making my way to the back. I was all alone, nearly to the creek when I started my search.

I spotted an egg hidden behind a small rock. I had to move fast. I wanted to win the bet.

I bent down, picked it up, and quickly dropped it in my basket.

Then I knelt down, set my basket on the ground, and started to search for more eggs.

But I jumped up when I heard a scream.

2

"Aaaaaiiiiii!"

The scream rang through the air.

I turned back toward the house. One of the Hair Sisters was waving her hand wildly, calling to the other girls. I grabbed up my basket and ran toward her.

"They're not hard-boiled!" I heard her cry as I came closer. And I saw the drippy yellow yolk running down the front of her white T-shirt.

"Mom didn't have time to hard-boil them," Brandy announced. "Or to paint them. I know it's weird. But there just wasn't time."

I raised my eyes to the house. Mom and Dad had both disappeared inside.

"Be careful," Brandy warned her party guests. "If you crack them —"

She didn't finish her sentence. I heard a wet *splat*.

Then laughter.

A boy had tossed an egg against the side of the doghouse.

"Cool!" one of the girls exclaimed.

Anne's big sheepdog, Stubby, came running out of the doghouse. I don't know why he likes to sleep in there. He's almost as big as the house.

But I didn't have time to think about Stubby.

Splat.

Another egg exploded, this time against the garage wall.

More laughter. Brandy's friends thought it was really hilarious.

"Egg fight! Egg fight!" two boys started to chant.

I ducked as an egg went sailing over my head. It landed with a *craaack* on the driveway.

Eggs were flying everywhere now. I stood there and gaped in amazement.

I heard a shrill shriek. I spun around to see that two of the Hair Sisters had runny yellow egg oozing in their hair. They were shouting and tugging at their hair and trying to pull the yellow gunk off with both hands.

Splat! Another egg hit the garage.

Craaack! Eggs bounced over the driveway.

I ducked down and searched from Anne. She probably went home, I figured. Anne enjoys a good laugh. But she's twelve, much too sophisticated for a babyish egg fight.

Well, then I'm wrong, I'm wrong.

"Think fast, Dana!" Anne screamed from behind me. I threw myself to the ground just in time. She heaved two eggs at once. They both whirred over my head and dropped onto the grass with a sickening *crack*.

"Stop it! Stop it!" I heard Brandy shrieking desperately. "It's my birthday! Stop it! It's my birthday!"

Thunnk! Somebody hit Brandy in the chest with an egg.

Wild laughter rang out. Sticky yellow puddles covered the back lawn.

I raised my eyes to Anne. She was grinning back at me, about to let me have it again.

Time for action. I reached into my basket and pulled out the one and only egg I had picked up.

I raised it high above my head. Started to throw — but stopped.

The egg.

I lowered it and stared at it.

Stared hard at it.

Something was wrong with the egg.

Something was terribly wrong.

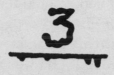

The egg was too big. Bigger than a normal egg. About the size of a softball.

I held it carefully, studying it. The color wasn't right either. It wasn't egg-colored. That creamy off-white. And it wasn't brown.

The egg was pale green. I raised it to the sunlight to make sure I was seeing correctly.

Yes. Green.

And what were those thick cracks up and down the shell?

I ran my pointer finger over the dark, jagged lines.

No. Not cracks. Some kind of veins. Blue-and-purple veins crisscrossing the green eggshell.

"Weird!" I muttered out loud.

Brandy's friends were shouting and shrieking. Eggs were flying all around me. An egg splattered over my sneakers. The yellow yolk oozed over my laces.

But I didn't care.

I rolled the strange egg over and over slowly between my hands. I brought it close to my face and squinted hard at the blue-and-purple veins.

"Ooh." I let out a low cry when I felt it pulsing. The veins throbbed. I could feel a steady beat. *Thud. Thud. Thud.*

"Oh wow. *It's alive!*" I cried.

What had I found? It was totally weird. I couldn't wait to get it to my worktable and examine it.

But first I had to show it to Anne.

"Anne! Hey — Anne!" I called and started jogging toward her, holding the egg high in both hands.

I was staring at the egg. So I didn't see Stubby, her big sheepdog, run in front of me.

"Whooooa!"

I let out a cry as I fell over the dog.

And landed with a sickening crunch on top of my egg.

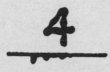

4

I jumped up quickly. Stubby started to lick my face. That dog has the *worst* breath!

I shoved him away and bent down to examine my egg.

"Hey!" I cried out in amazement. The egg wasn't broken. I picked it up carefully and rolled it in my hands.

Not a crack.

What a tough shell! I thought. My chest had landed on top of the egg. Pushed it into the ground. But the shell hadn't broken.

I wrapped my hands around the big egg as if soothing it.

I could feel the blue-and-purple veins pulsing.

Is something inside getting ready to hatch? I wondered. What kind of bird was inside it? Not a chicken, I knew. This was definitely not a hen's egg.

Splat!

Another egg smacked the side of the garage. Kids were wrestling in the runny puddles of yolk on the grass. I turned in time to see a boy crack an egg over another boy's head.

"Stop it! Stop it!"

Brandy was screaming at the top of her lungs, trying to stop the egg fight before every single egg was smashed. I turned and saw Mom and Dad running across the yard.

"Hey, Anne —!" I called. I climbed to my feet, holding the weird egg carefully. Anne was frantically tossing eggs at three girls. The girls were bombarding her. Three to one — but Anne wasn't retreating.

"Anne — check this out!" I called, hurrying over to her. "You won't believe this egg!"

I stepped up beside her and held the egg out to her.

"No! Wait —!" I cried.

Too late.

Anne grabbed my egg and heaved it at the three girls.

5

"No — stop!" I wailed.

As I stared in horror, one of the three girls caught the egg in midair — and tossed it back.

I dove for it, making a headfirst slide. And grabbed the egg in one hand before it hit the gravel.

Was it broken?

No.

This shell must be made of steel! I told myself. I pulled myself to my feet, gripping the egg carefully. To my surprise, it felt hot. Burning hot.

"Whoa!" I nearly dropped it.

Throb. Throb. Throb.

It pulsed rapidly. I could feel the veins beating against my fingers.

I wanted to show the egg to Mom and Dad. But they were busy breaking up the egg fight.

Dad's face was bright red. He was shouting at

Brandy and pointing to the yellow stains up and down the side of the garage.

Mom was trying to calm down two girls who were crying. They had egg yolk stuck to their hair and all over their clothes. They even had it stuck to their eyebrows. I guess that's why they were crying.

Behind them Stubby was having a feast. He was running around in circles, lapping up egg after egg from the grass, his bushy tail wagging like crazy.

What a party!

I decided to take my weird egg inside. I wanted to study it later. Maybe I'd break off a tiny piece of shell and look at it under the microscope. Then I'd make a tiny hole in the shell and try to see inside.

Throb. Throb.

The veins pounded against my hand. The egg still felt hot.

It might be a turtle egg, I decided. I walked carefully to the house, cradling it in both hands.

One morning last fall Anne found a big box turtle on the curb in front of her house. She carried it into her backyard and called me over. She knew I'd want to study it.

It was a pretty big turtle. About the size of a lunch box. Anne and I wondered how it got to her curb.

Up in my room I had a book about turtles. I knew the book would help me identify it. I hurried home to get the book. But Mom wouldn't let me go back out. I had to stay inside and have lunch.

When I got back to Anne's backyard, the turtle had vanished. I guess it wandered away.

Turtles can be pretty fast when they want to be.

As I carried my treasure into the house, I thought it might be a turtle egg. But why was it so hot? And why did it have those yucky veins all over it?

Eggs don't have veins — do they?

I hid the egg in my dresser drawer. I surrounded it with my balled-up socks to protect it. Then I closed the drawer slowly, carefully, and returned to the backyard.

Brandy's guests were all leaving as I stepped outside. They were covered in sticky eggs. They didn't look too happy.

Brandy didn't look too happy, either. Dad was busy shouting at her, angrily waving his arms, pointing to the gloppy egg stains all over the lawn.

"Why did you let this happen?" he screamed at her. "Why didn't you stop it?"

"I tried!" Brandy wailed. "I tried to stop it!"

"We'll have to have the garage painted," Mom murmured, shaking her head. "How will we ever mow the lawn?"

"This was the worst party I ever had!" Brandy cried. She bent down and pulled chunks of eggshell from her sneaker laces. Then she glared up at Mom. "It's all *your* fault!"

"Huh?" Mom gasped. "My fault?"

"You didn't hard-boil the eggs," Brandy accused. "So it's all your fault."

Mom started to protest — but bit her lip instead.

Brandy stood up and tossed the bits of eggshell to the ground. She flashed Mom her best dimpled smile. "Next year for my birthday, can we have a Make-Your-Own Ice-Cream Sundae party?"

That evening I wanted to study my weird green egg. But we had to go visit Grandma Evelyn and Grandpa Harry and take them out to dinner. They always make a big fuss about Brandy's birthday.

First, Brandy had to open her presents. Grandma Evelyn bought her a pair of pink fuzzy slippers that Brandy will never wear. She'll probably give them to Stubby as chew toys.

Brandy opened the biggest box next. She pulled out a pair of pink and white pajamas. Brandy made a big fuss about them and said she really needed pajamas. She did a pretty good acting job.

But how excited can you get over pajamas?

Her last present was a twenty-five-dollar gift certificate to the CD store at the mall. Nice presents. "I'll go with you to make sure you don't pick out anything lame," I offered.

Brandy pretended she didn't hear me.

She gave our grandparents big hugs. Brandy is a big hugger. Then we all went out for dinner at the new Italian restaurant on the corner.

What did we talk about at dinner? Brandy's wild birthday party. When we told Grandma and Grandpa about the egg fight, they laughed and laughed.

It wasn't so funny in the afternoon. But a few hours later at dinner, we all had to admit it was pretty funny. Even Dad managed a smile or two.

I kept thinking about the egg in my dresser drawer. When we got back home, would I find a baby turtle on my socks?

Dinner stretched on and on. Grandpa Harry told all of his funny golfing stories. He tells them every time we visit. We always laugh anyway.

We didn't return home till really late. Brandy fell asleep in the car. And I could barely keep my eyes open.

I slunk up to my room and changed into pajamas. Then, with a loud yawn, I turned off the light. I knew I'd fall asleep the moment my head hit the pillow.

I fluffed my pillow the way I liked it. Then I slid into bed and pulled the quilt up to my chin.

I started to settle my head on the pillow when I heard the sound.

Thump. Thump. Thump.

Steady like a heartbeat. Only louder.

Much louder.

THUMP. THUMP. THUMP.

So loud, I could hear the dresser drawers rattling.

I sat straight up. Wide awake now, I stared through the darkness to my dresser.

THUMP. THUMP. THUMP.

I turned and lowered my feet to the floor.

Should I open the dresser drawer?

I sat in the darkness, trembling with excitement. With fear.

Listening to the steady thud.

Should I open the drawer and check it out?

Or should I run as far away as I could?

About the Author

R.L. STINE is the author of the series *Fear Street, Nightmare Room, Give Yourself Goosebumps,* and the phenomenally successful *Goosebumps.* His thrilling teen titles have sold more than 250 million copies internationally — enough to earn him a spot in the *Guinness Book of World Records*! Mr. Stine lives in New York City with his wife, Jane, and his son, Matt.